Sally was beside herself with rage!

And she was totally unprepared when Lyle's arms snaked around her waist and drew her to him.

"Am I supposed to say you're beautiful when you're angry?" he asked with husky amusement. "Well, you are, Sally Brown. Very beautiful... with that yellow spark in your green eyes, skin as soft as a spring flower, a mouth made for a man's kisses...."

She stiffened, her hands pushing against shoulders that were immovable, but the provocative trail of his fingers over her hair and down in a tracing motion over her cheek and neck, left her without breath to make her protest. His hands ran strokingly down her back, shivering awareness to life and bringing her trembling lips up to receive the teasing pressure of his mouth.

ELIZABETH GRAHAM

stormy vigil

Harlequin Books

TORONTO • NEW YORK • LOS ANGELES • LONDON
AMSTERDAM • PARIS • SYDNEY • HAMBURG
STOCKHOLM • ATHENS • TOKYO • MILAN

Harlequin Presents first edition November 1982
ISBN 0-373-10543-6

Original hardcover edition published in 1982
by Mills & Boon Limited

CHAPTER ONE

THE metallic clang of rapid-fire typewriters greeted Sally Brown as she stepped from the tiny cubicle laughingly referred to as her office and into the main throb of *Northwest Then and Now*. The photo magazine, barely two years old and suffering the pangs of any newborn publication, provided no frills for its photo journalists. Even Jerry Pelham, its overall president, boasted no more than six extra feet of office space and a view of Seattle's lesser downtown core.

But plush surroundings had been the least of Sally's concern when, a graduate of her university's course in journalism, she had been sought out by Jerry to be part of the team on the new magazine he was starting. She wasn't that naïve about the business world that Jerry's choice should have fallen on her, a fledgling in journalism. The plain fact was that her services came a lot cheaper than someone with hard experience under their belt. She was an unknown quality, but the bright determination that had marked her university days made her recognise that *Northwest Then and Now* was but a step to the brilliant career she planned for herself.

Bypassing Jerry's faultlessly made up secretary, she tapped lightly at his door and walked into his office. Her eyes went briefly round the walls decorated with cover layouts of previous issues and blow-ups of prominent Seattle citizens featured in the articles before coming round to rest on the cluttered desk of the magazine's owner.

Slightly built and with hair the colour of burnished corn, Jerry Pelham possessed all the attributes of an up-and-coming executive. His suits were immaculately tailored, his linen fresh and crisp, and his tie knotted at just the right angle. An attractive man by any woman's standards, and Sally knew that many women forgot virtue and scruples where Jerry was concerned. Strangely, her own attitude of business before pleasure seemed to titillate his amorous senses. Heaven knew, she was no raving beauty. But what she did have was a breezy self-confidence in her own worth, a confidence reflected in the clean shine of her shoulder-length brown hair, the bright sparkle in her greenish-hazel eyes, the slender figure she dressed with taste.

'You wanted to see me?' she asked, her voice pitched to unaware attractiveness in her husky tone.

'I always want to see you, Sally, you know that.' Jerry waved a hand to the chairs opposite his desk and Sally sank gracefully into the one on his left side. Maybe it was his eyes, she reflected fleetingly as she smoothed the skirt of her camel suit over her knees. Bulbous, palely blue, they dominated without force. Not that she wanted, needed, the outdated *macho* image that had made women slaves to their domineering husbands in times past. Her preference would be for a man as confident of his maleness as she was of her femininity, and somehow Jerry didn't fit that bill.

'And I'm always available,' she said evenly, 'for business.'

'Business—yes.' His nod was speculative as his eyes rested on her. Enthusiasm spiked his voice as he went on, 'How would you like to land the plum of interviewing our State Governor at his Twin Oaks estate? He's given permission for us to attend his annual ball there just before Christmas as well as a couple of interviews before that to give us some highlights on his family history. You know how prominent his family has been in Washington's history, from pioneer smallholder to Chief Executive of the State.'

Sally stared uncomprehendingly at him, her eyes a darkened moss green as his words sank into her brain. 'How can I cover that?' she said at last. 'I'm in the middle of my lighthouse project, and that has to be completed before the Christmas issue.'

'Lighthouses? Oh, my God, Sally, don't you understand what these interviews with the Governor can mean? They're important, and the lighthouse project isn't.'

'It is to me,' Sally insisted stubbornly. 'I've spent two months visiting the lighthouses round our shores, staying with the keepers and their families, getting to know them and the problems they have—there's only one left to do, Jerry, for heaven's sake!' she ended on a dismal wail.

'One?' he asked sharply. 'When is that scheduled?'

'December the fifteenth,' she responded through gritted teeth. The lighthouse project had become something meaningful to her in her travels along Washington State's coastline. In these days of automation there were few manned lighthouses left and the few remaining ones, in her opinion, personified all that the magazine sought to portray. 'This is different, it's a completely isolated lump of rock set in the most treacherous waters our State knows. The family that runs it now,' she leaned forward in desperation, 'has been there for forty years or more. It's a kind of father-to-son operation, because the son of the man who worked the lighthouse in the years after the second World War is carrying on in his father's footsteps.'

Jerry seemed to retreat from her as he leaned back in the brown leather expanse of his office chair and regarded her narrowly. 'It's a good story,' he acknowledged, 'but this one's even better. However, they don't have to overlap, do they? You can do the preliminary interviews with the Governor and his family before leaving for the lighthouse one on the fifteenth. It shouldn't take too long to cover that, and you'll be back long before the Governor's levee on December twenty-third.'

That was as far as Jerry was prepared to go on the strict time limit the magazine's production date stipulated, and Sally was still fuming as she retraced her steps to the partitioned area off the main office that she called her own.

The lighthouse project had become important to her over the past few weeks. Getting to know the keepers and their families, probing their reasons for choosing that kind of isolation, had opened her up personally, given her a widened view of life lived on a different level from her own. Since she had lived all her life in an urban environment, it had come as something of a shock to her to realise that some people—very special people—had depths to their character that sustained the lonely hours when often their only human contact was with the lights of grateful ships passing through a treacherous stretch of channel in safety because of the beacon the keeper kept brightly shining.

Rock Island, the last on her list, was the most isolated, the most important lighthouse in a chain that dotted the Washington shoreline. Unlike the other stations she had visited on the coast, this one would necessitate a visit of several days. But, having come to know, like and respect the keepers in other areas, she had no qualms about getting along with the Hemmings of Rock Island.

Hemming, she mused, leaning back in her padded round chair and staring contemplatively at the ceiling. Lyle Hemming was a professor of English at university, a tall, lean-faced and dark-haired faculty member who had set his students' hearts beating at an incredible level. She herself had been in none of his classes, but there wasn't a girl on campus who didn't recognise the long-legged stride of the English professor or the fact that he had no domestic entanglements. Not that his single status made him more available to the enamoured students in his care. According to the grapevine whose gossip swept the campus like a forest fire, Lyle Hemming preferred older, more experienced women, such as the dynamic blonde Sally herself had seen him with at the exclusive Harvey's Club on a visit there with her parents. She remembered thinking at the time that the desirable Professor Hemming must make a fetish of being unavailable—the more the blonde pressed, the more he seemed to retreat.

Reminiscence faded abruptly from her eyes as her door was thrust open and Jerry's energetic figure catapulted into the room.

'It's all fixed up,' he told her triumphantly. 'There's a family gathering next week, and you're invited, then there's an exclusive interview including a tour of the house on the tenth.'

'Oh,' Sally blinked dully. 'You mean the Governor thing.'

Jerry's stare was impatient. 'Of course the Governor thing. What's more important than that? I can put somebody else on the lighthouse series if you——'

'No,' she cut in hastily, 'I can make all of them.'

'Do you want a photographer?'

'What? Oh, no.' Sally gave him a belated indignant look. 'I usually do my own photography, you know that.'

'Sure,' he dismissed, 'but this is something special. On second thoughts, I'm going to assign Dave to the project. He knows what he's doing.'

'And I don't?'

'I'm not saying that, but I'd be happier if you have Dave to back you up.'

When Jerry used that tone of voice there was no arguing with him, and Sally shrugged her shoulders as he went from the room. Dave Fisher was nice, a professional to his fingertips despite his youth. She would enjoy working with him on the Governor project.

'This is Nathaniel's wife's work,' the Governor's wife enthused gently. 'While he hewed out what was to be Trent farms, Emily made her own mark

in the district. It was she who set the moral tone,
who worked diligently for the establishment of
standards which exist to this day. She lived an ex-
emplary life, and expected everyone around her to
do so as well.'

I can believe that, Sally told herself silently as
her eyes went from the neat stitching of a framed
quilt to the clear, straightforward, yet somehow
cold look of the woman whose portrait took pre-
cedence over the quilt. Not a woman to look kindly
on the frailties of human nature, those lifeless eyes
proclaimed. How different she and her husband
had been, she thought involuntarily, recalling the
wicked gleam in Nathaniel Trent's eyes as they
leapt from the canvas.

If the truth were told, this assignment bored her.
The people concerned possessed little of the attraction of the lighthouse-keepers. They were real
people, surviving and being happy under difficult
conditions. The Trents might have survived—obviously they had—but happily? Emily's dour coun-
tenance denied any such supposition.

While Dave dutifully took pictures of the noble
old house and its present occupants, Sally's
thoughts ranged far away. In her mind's eye she
composed the beginning of her article on the remotest of all the lighthouses, Rock Island. 'Set far
away from the amenities of civilised life, the light
station on Rock Island——' That was as far as she
could go without actually meeting the people who
lived there—the Hemmings. What motivated a
woman to give up the civilised conveniences and
live with her man in such a remote spot, with only
him for company? A special kind of woman, like

the ones she had met on other isolated stations, she decided, smiling abstractedly as she followed her hostess from house to gardens.

Back at her own apartment later that evening she went, drink in hand, to the narrow balcony doors with their slivered view of grey ocean, and her thoughts went once more to Rock Island. This wasn't the best time to pay a visit to a storm-swept light station, when the Pacific, belying its name, could hold many of the terrors associated with its sister ocean, the Atlantic. But, true daughter of her father, an ardent yachtsman, as Sally was, the turbulent ocean held little fear for her. How often had she crewed for him on this same ocean, setting the jib on his sleek racing yacht?

Her thoughts jagged off in time to the days when those sea trips with her father were the highlight of her life. Tall, bronzed, capable, no man had ever come near Jesse Brown's influence over his daughter. Many had tried, but none had succeeded in replacing his perfect image in her eyes. Nor had any other woman come close to taking the place of Stella Brown, her mother, whose paintings of the Pacific Northwest were beginning to be discovered elsewhere in the country. Sally's upbringing had perhaps been unconventional, but it had made of her a woman aware of the subleties of humour applied to the everyday occurrences in life, the tolerance of views not her own, an ability to think and live free within her own personal boundaries.

'You're just *too* damned independent!' an erstwhile suitor had once told her, and she guessed that was so. Sighing as she leaned on the painted wood of the patio doors, she conceded that what he said was true. She had her own thoughts, her own dreams, about the man who would one day dominate her life. As enlightened as herself, he would accept the freeness of her spirit and recognise her own need to be a person in her own right, separate from the love that bound them ... Turning back from the window, Sally went with a nervous stride into the skylit kitchen where her self-made dinner of lasagna in spicy sauce bubbled joyfully in the glass-fronted oven. A meal fit for the gods, only there was no god to share it with her. Sighing, she flicked off the heat on the stove and extracted the reddish-gold Italian style dish from the oven. Not for the first time, she regretted the absence of another person to share it with ... a man who would praise the subtle tastes of garlic, tomato paste, spices that recalled the unique flavour of Southern Italy....

Alone, for some reason feeling desolate, she ate the meal designed for two....

'Is it always this rough?' she enquired of the boatman who, days later, transported her to the island whose outlines became misty in the trailing wisps of fog as the snub-nosed boat ploughed its way through whitecapped waves that seemed determined to keep the trim craft away from the rocky foreshore that was their destination.

Sally checked again the waterproof covers of the camera equipment tucked down beside her. Just as she ascertained that the delicate lenses were immune to the salt spray drenching the aft deck of the sturdy boat, its owner disparaged.

'Hell, this is nothing. I've seen Rock Island in

worse conditions than this, although——' his lined
sea-blue eyes searched the misting clouds on the
far horizon—'this could blow up to quite a squall.
You said they're expecting you?' he swivelled
momentarily from his stance at the rain-slicked
wheel.

'Yes, yes, they know I'm coming,' she returned
impatiently, her eyes straining to reach the storm-
washed rocks dead ahead. This really was the
lighthouse to end all lighthouses, and she hoped
sourly that Jerry would appreciate the hazards she
had encountered in reaching the desolate outpost.

Speculation died as Rock Island suddenly
became real, a grey entity in its own right, seemingly devoid of landing places among the sea-
washed rocks that made it an impregnable fortress.
But the boatman, veteran of many such trips,
manoeuvred the small craft to the lee side of the
jutting rocks while Sally's gaze rose to the soaring
edifice above them. Banded by spiralling red
stripes, the lighthouse commanded an imposing
position above the stark promontory of grey rock
jutting out into the rising whitecaps washing
against the weathered grey at its foot.

Her landing on the small jetty was un-
prepossessing, to say the least. Awaiting the surging swell that hesitated momentarily at its crest,
the boatman propelled her on to the weathered
boards and tossed her seaman-type bag after her.
Feeling strangely deserted, she watched numbly as
he pulled away from the dock in a wide circle
before heading back to the mainland they had
come from.

'You be sure to come back for me on Thursday!'

she shouted into the wind, and wasn't sure if he had heard her or not, although he waved in friendly fashion as the boat began its battle with the oncoming swell.

Her eyes lifted to the jagged outline of seasoned rock surrounding the colourfully striped lighthouse. A moment of unrealistic panic swept her in the realisation that no one had come to meet her. The Hemmings knew she was arriving that day, surely they would have been watching for the boat that carried her. Were these the keepers destined to destroy her happy impression of the friendly, hospitable souls who manned these bastions of the Republic?

Her fingers, chilled despite their covering of sheepskin gloves, took hold of the woven carrying loop on her bag, and she adjusted the camera equipment more evenly across her shoulders. The Hemmings, she told herself as she trudged towards the balconied steps leading upward, could be forgiven for missing the arrival of a small boat at their landing pier. The weather, worsening by the minute, must have kept their awareness concentrated on the work they had been hired to do. Keeping a lighthouse in functional order required vigilance, even in these days of automation.

Wind snatched her breath away as she mounted higher on the solidly constructed steps to the summit. Her eyes went to the swirling waters sucking hungrily at the rocks far below, then swivelled back to the staircase she was climbing. Now wasn't the time to unearth all the fears lurking at the back of a person's mind, however skilled they were in marine navigation. Giving herself a respite, Sally paused on a landing and looked up again to the forbidding outline of stratified rock. Even her father might have felt trepidation in facing the uncertainty of the ocean's power to destroy in that setting.

Belittling herself for giving in to the fears that must have attacked the keepers of this lighthouse many times, she kept her eyes resolutely on the next flight of stairs, the next landing, telling herself that the survival of the Hemming family proved the invincibility of Rock Island's fortress-like impregnability to the forces of nature raging far below.

The winds sang and taunted her eardrums as she ascended the final, mercifully short, climb to the rocky plateau housing the lighthouse. The dizzy, euphoric feeling of having conquered the elements dissipated rapidly when a harsh voice, far from the welcoming warmth she had been expecting, said explosively,

'Who are you, and what the hell are you doing here?'

Her eyes focused dimly on a belligerent figure placed slightly above and to the right. All-weather boots gave rise to long male legs encased snugly in clay-coloured pants of firmly woven twill, a jacket of padded brown nylon embracing shoulders a lumberjack wouldn't be ashamed to own. But it was his face—a high-planed, hard-jawed edifice seemingly hewn from the rocks surrounding them—that drew her attention.

Faintness sent numbing fingers of dullness over her senses. She knew that face as well as any female student who had ever yearned over him.

Professor Hemming!—Luke Hemming, the English professor at university who made hearts beat faster in idealistic co-ed breasts! Sally spared a fleeting moment to wonder if the love throbbing in those breasts would last if they could see his harshly unwelcome visage now, but flooding in after that was her own bewilderment at being faced with, not the lighthouse keeper she had expected, but a man whose field of endeavour was far removed from these rugged shores.

'I'm here to interview Mr John Hemming and his family for *Northwest Then and Now*,' she explained crisply, albeit breathlessly from the long climb. Seeing his quick frown of uncomprehension, she went on, 'They're expecting me. Would you please take me to him? It's not exactly comfortable standing here with a gale force wind buffeting us.'

A wind that tugged at her pile-lined suede jacket and tossed the dark strands of Lyle Hemming's hair across his broad forehead in a disconcerting way.

As if her words had only now drawn his attention to the raging power of the wind, he gestured with an ungloved hand towards the neatly trimmed white house nestled behind the dominating height of the lighthouse. 'You'd better come with me,' he said abruptly, making no attempt to assume her luggage burden as he strode off along the lichen-covered rock. For a moment Sally stared sourly after him, then she stooped and took up her bag again as she followed his broad male shoulders in the direction of the squatly set house sheltered by the thrusting column of the lighthouse.

Natural rock formed an uneven pathway to the

residence, and Sally's reporter's mind registered the tubbed greenery of spruce and pine lining the walkway while her brain registered more important data. Lyle Hemming must be related to the John Hemming who was responsible for the lighthouse, but why should Lyle be here during an academic year when, she reflected drily as she followed him into the minuscule hallway, he should be reaping the full benefit of the female English majors from this year's crop of university students?

Enlightenment came when, after divesting herself of jacket and hanging it on the row of pegs provided in the hall, she followed him into a well furnished living room where a log fire sparked benignly in its surrounds of white-painted rock.

'My brother and his wife had to leave suddenly because of illness with one of their kids,' Lyle Hemming explained briefly, stationing himself like an inquisitor before the broad fireplace and staring unblinkingly at Sally with eyes the colour of topaz. 'I presume they expected your visit?'

'Yes, yes, they did,' Sally summoned her low-cadenced voice. 'I'm Sally Brown from the *Northwest Now and Then* magazine. I'm doing a series on lighthouses, and I——'

'Sally Brown?' he echoed, ignoring the information she had proffered after giving her name. 'Your parents obviously didn't have too much imagination when they chose your name.'

'My parents are the most imaginative people I know,' she retorted coolly, moving closer to the reflected heat of the fireplace while still avoiding the spare leanness of the figure dominating it. 'They're also down-to-earth, practical people. They

didn't burden me with "Clarissa" or "Rosamund".
My mother has functioned quite happily under her
name of Stella.'

'Stella Brown? The painter?' he ejaculated incredulously, his sweeping gaze taking in the form
of her shape, somewhat ungainly under the enveloping moss green of her loose-fitting sweater.

'Stella's my mother, yes,' she said offhandedly,
wondering at her own need to coast on her
mother's reputation. It wasn't often that she traded
on Stella's fame, but something about this man and
his coldly clinical air made her want to seek im-
portance in his eyes ... even the secondhand im-
portance of a mother who had made her name in a
field Sally wouldn't, couldn't, aspire to.

'She's very talented,' Lyle Hemming commented
now, confirming the opinion of numerous art
critics who had appraised her mother's works. His
pleasantly based voice took on a mocking tone.
'And what about your father? Is he content to live
in your mother's shadow?'

Irritation prickled along Sally's veins. 'He
doesn't have to,' she bit off abruptly, wishing ferv-
ently that she could walk out on this man who had
all the confidence of several years' tenure on his
professorial job at the university. 'He's won several
awards for his building projects in Seattle.'

'Jesse Brown, the architect?' he mused, less
questioning than wondering as his brown-hued
gaze went over Sally once again. 'So you're the
product of two exceptionally talented people?'

Defensive in a way she had never known before,
Sally bit off the words that rose heatedly to her
throat and confined herself to, 'The jury's still out

on whether I qualify to be the daughter of two such talented people. Is it permissible for me to ask just what a professor of English is doing way out here in the middle of nowhere?'

'I'll tell you about that when I've made us some tea,' he responded blandly, his long legs moving powerfully as he crossed the room and paused at its doorway. 'I'm presuming you don't prefer something stronger—my brother keeps a fairly extensive bar for visitors with more exotic tastes.'

'Tea will be fine,' she told him coolly, although as his well-knit form disappeared in the direction of what she assumed was the kitchen her jangling nerves told her that an alcoholic drink wouldn't have gone amiss. Her arrival on Rock Island had met none of her imaginings on the subject. Rotating on the heels of her fine leather boots, she stared contemplatively at the glowing centre of the log fire.

John Hemming and his wife, her expected hosts, were not here. Equally obvious was the fact that Lyle Hemming, John's brother, was in sole charge of the light station. A quick glance towards the double-paned glass of the living room windows assured her that night would fall within the hour, leaving her trapped in this rocky bastion with a man she distrusted for some reason. Her eyes came back into the room and rested briefly, lightly, on the inexpensive prints lining the walls, the brass collection of a woman cut off from the normal amenities of life. Maybe there was an assistant keeper, a younger man serving his probationary time on this remote lighthouse before taking on the responsibility of his own station. Wasn't it a rule that a lighthouse should be manned by at least two people who knew what they were doing?

Relieved at the thought, Sally turned to face the man who came back into the cosy sitting room bearing a tray set with tea things. His dark hair took on a burnished glow from the fire as he set the tray down on the low table between two fireside chairs.

'It looks as if I'll have to spend at least one night here,' she indicated with her head the darkening terrain outside the windows, 'but I can probably get most of the information I need from the assistant lightkeeper. When does he come off duty?'

Lyle Hemming's eyes lifted to meet hers, something in their brown depths striking a chill down her backbone. 'The assistant lightkeeper is a she, not he,' he informed her as he straightened, 'and she went with her husband to be with their sick child.'

Sally's eyes gleamed in the flickering fireglow as she stared across at the English professor. 'You mean——?' she stammered uncharacteristically, 'your brother's wife is the—the *assistant*?'

'That's it, in a nutshell,' he said matter-of-factly, his eyes hard as they faced hers across the low table. 'Lorna is qualified to take over when John can't for any reason.'

'But—but what happens in a case like this?' Sally got out, her eyes fastened critically on the man opposite. 'Surely somebody responsible should be left in charge?'

'Somebody responsible *has* been left in charge.' Lyle Hemming bent casually down to the table and lifted the china teapot. 'Don't forget I was brought up on this lighthouse. I know every nook and cranny of this godforsaken rock. I know what to do when conditions are normal, and I can make a pretty accurate stab at what to do when nature decides to play rough. What's the matter, Miss Brown? Afraid I'll let the fog swallow you up?'

'There's no fog,' she asserted nervously, turning to the windows to reassure herself nonetheless. The lowering clouds that cast darkness on the rocks surrounding them did nothing to dispel her sudden apprehension. 'I'll go back to the mainland in the morning,' she said nervously, 'and get my story from your brother and his wife at a later time.

Dark gold liquid spouted from the china pot Lyle Hemming held in a sparsely fleshed hand. 'You can forget about going back to the mainland,' he told her dispassionately, 'for at least a week.'

'A week?' Sally's gasp was followed quickly by a clearcut vision of Jerry's face when she failed to turn up for the Governor's Levee. 'That's silly, I have to be back for—for other assignments long before that.'

'Can't be done,' Lyle Hemming stated calmly as he handed her a delicately fluted china cup, his capably contoured hands manipulating the fine porcelain as if he were presiding over a faculty tea party. Declining the milk and sugar he proferred but accepting his waved offer of the chair behind her, Sally sank, cup in hand, into its upholstered depths, trying desperately to marshal her thoughts into some kind of order.

It was absolutely impossible that she should stay here alone on this bleakly isolated rock for a week with Lyle Hemming as her only companion. Yet it

seemed that was what she would have to do if his
prognostication about the weather was correct. If
only it had been some other man—Jerry, even, or
Dave. She had something in common with them in
their work. Jerry might have tried taking advantage
of the situation in a personal fashion, but she could
have handled him in the normal way. Lyle
Hemming was totally out of her sphere of experience, and she realised now as she looked thoughtfully at him over the rim of her cup that she had
always faintly despised him and his type. Colour
ran up under her cheeks when his yellow-brown
gaze disconcertingly met hers.

'Yes,' he read her thoughts with mocking accur-
acy, 'you're trapped here with the Don Juan of
English Lit. Does that fact strike terror into your
prissy little soul?'

Sally gasped, not so much for the venom in his
last words but because he apparently recognised
her from her years at college. 'I—I didn't think
you'd ever—noticed me,' she stammered lamely,
realising that she sounded surprisingly like the
smitten co-eds under his tutelage, but unable to do
anything about it.

'Oh, I noticed you.' He laid his cup on the tray
and stood up, thrusting his hands into his trouser
pockets and stretching the beige material over flatly
contoured hips while the fire warmed his back.
'You stood out like a sore thumb, if you'll pardon
the cliché, among the fluttery-eyed female students
it was my futile task to teach.' A grim smile
touched his full-shaped lips as he looked down into
Sally's perplexed eyes. 'I should have known you'd
turn out to be the one who'd use your English in-

struction creatively.'

'Dr Jeffreys was good at his job, and he had the added advantage of being in his sixties and perfectly content with his wife of forty years,' she sparked waspishly.

'What would you have me do? Scar my face with acid and marry some addlepated woman who'd drive me mad in three days?'

Compelled forcefully to look at the situation from his point of view, Sally conceded that it might be difficult for a young, attractive teacher without ties to fend off the adulation teenage girls indulged in, but surely——

'All women are not addlepated, as you called them,' she defended, 'in fact most women, once they're past the age of swooning over idols, are reasonable, intelligent human beings. Surely you're not trying to tell me that out of all the women you've known, there hasn't been one you——'

'There was one, yes,' he conceded briefly, nodding stiffly, 'but she was one in a class of her own.' A frown that might have connoted pain was still etched sharply into his brow when he went on briskly, 'If you've finished your tea, I'll take you up to where you'll be sleeping.' At the door he paused and swivelled to face her. 'Can you cook?'

'Reasonably—why?' Sally replaced her cup on the tray and stood up, her eyes innocently puzzled as they went to his across the narrow space of the small room.

'Because it's not my forte,' he bit off the words sharply. 'So unless you're prepared for a diet of canned chilli beans you'd better make use of the freezer Lorna keeps well stocked. The only fresh vegetable we have is potatoes; apart from that we live on the frozen variety.'

'You mean the god of Lit. 214 has feet of clay?' she mocked, moving across to stand in front of him. 'You surprise me. I wouldn't have thought you'd admit to inadequacy in any department.'

A flicker that could have been amusement crossed his eyes, dispelling the heavy frown. 'I don't. In any department.'

The flat emphasis in his tone left no doubt in Sally's mind as to his meaning and she cursed inwardly as hotness flamed her cheeks again. Why had she felt the need to climb on her high horse where this man was concerned? He had forgotten more masterful strokes of repartee than she would ever learn. Damn him!

'Shall we go?' she suggested with a hint of sweet forbearance, and after a barely perceptible pause, he turned. Following him across the minuscule hallway and up the staircase at its side which rose steeply to the upper level, she wished she could ignore the neat conformation of his hips, the powerful length of his legs. Her fellow students hadn't overestimated his attractions. He was a devastating mixture of sheer male potency and cerebral brilliance.

Doors stood open to the four small bedrooms opening off a narrow passage, and the Professor led her into a single-bedded tiny room opposite what was obviously the master bedroom.

'It's small,' he echoed her thought, his eyes running appraisingly over her neat frame, 'but then you are, too. I've taken over John and Lorna's room, single beds aren't roomy enough for me.'

Sally involuntarily pictured in her mind's eye the bed he would own in the city. Acres big, spread with red-tinted fur, and probably surrounded by mirrors for titilating views of what went on there. Lyle Hemming, Agent 007!

'My bag,' she said distractedly, turning to find him squarely set in the narrow doorway, his eyes softly mocking as if he had once again been party to her thoughts. 'If you'll stand aside, I'll get it.'

Furthering his implacable image, he crossed his arms over his substantial chest and stared disconcertingly at her. She was conscious suddenly of the windswept untidiness of her hair, of lips that must be unnaturally pale without the pastel covering of gloss, the baggy contours of her shape-shrouding sweater. The knowledge that she was truly alone with a man who digested others of her sex with his breakfast cornflakes ran over her with renewed clarity. Why had she come here?—why hadn't she let Jerry send someone, preferably male, in her place as he had suggested?

'Will you please let me pass?' she threw back her head to say, though the note of panic in her voice must have been just as obvious to him as it was to herself, because he dropped his arms and said contemptuously,

'Don't get hysterical on me, for God's sake. I'm not in the habit of forcing myself on defenceless females, whatever your opinion of my character. I'll get your bag,' he ended abruptly, and seconds later she heard the thud of his feet on the steep staircase.

An uncontrollable tremor was still shaking her when he came back and brushed past her to deposit the canvas bag on the white hobnailed bedspread, but he appeared not to notice that as he went back to the door and flicked a cold glance at her.

'I have to go over to the tower and make some recordings, but I'll be back to make a meal for us. You can take over your share tomorrow.'

Sally stood immobile long after his feet had retraced their steps down the stairs and the front door slammed decisively behind him. She had obviously hurt him—no, *offended* him, with her fears. And she guessed that Lyle Hemming wasn't the man to forget or forgive any wound to his integrity.

CHAPTER TWO

IT was an hour later when Sally, lured by the aroma wafting upstairs from the lower regions, went hesitantly down the narrow staircase. At its foot she paused and glanced into the living room with its newly replenished fire and, finding it empty, let her gaze wander to the back of the hall where an open door made no barrier to the sound of china being set out.

Running a hand over the soft fall of her hair although she had brushed it only moments before, she took the step or two that brought her to the kitchen entrance. The Professor, looking cosily at home in domestic surroundings, much to her surprise, was standing back from a red checked covered table, frowning as his eyes went over the cutlery and glassware set out there. Muttering an exclamation, he turned to the sturdy Welsh dresser along the far wall and extracted paper napkins from one of its drawers.

'Can I help?' Sally took a step into the kitchen and wondered if she only imagined the flicker of irritation in his eyes as he looked up from his task at the table. His glance was all encompassing, taking in the washed freshness of her face and the re-application of the light make-up she used, as well as the pale green sweater which was much more figure-defining than the one she had arrived in.

'No,' he said abruptly, 'it's just about ready. If you'll go into the sitting room, I'll bring us some wine.'

'Wine?' Her eyes went involuntarily round the homely kitchen with its propane cookstove and substantial refrigerator, the rustic charm of the plate-decorated dresser.

'We're not entirely uncivilised,' he said drily turning to take glasses from the dresser's capacious lower half. 'Why is it presumed that because people live in isolation they can't enjoy the finer side of life?'

'Did I say that?'

'You didn't have to. You have the most transparent expression I've ever seen on a woman.' Taking the chilled wine from the refrigerator, he poured two healthy servings and came towards her purposefully, a glass in either hand. 'Shall we go?' he said pointedly, and Sally spun on her heel.

How she hated his sardonic male arrogance! she fumed as she led the way into the small sitting room. For no better reason than that countless students under his care had made simpering fools of themselves, he had set himself up as an authority on the female sex. Sinking into the chair she had used earlier, she accepted the glass of wine from his hand without grace.

There was an uneasy silence while Sally stared hard-eyed into the flames now leaping voraciously in the fireplace. Conscious of his puzzled downward glance, she steadfastly refused to return it until he spoke quietly.

'My remark was meant as a compliment. Most women spend a lot of time cloaking their reactions with a curtain of mystery, and it's refreshing to find one who doesn't feel that's necessary.'

Taken aback by the sincerity in his tone, Sally's eyes lifted to the tigerish yellow gleam in his, but didn't stop there. They wandered up to the thick vitality of his dark hair and the vagrant strand that fell casually over his wide-spaced brow, and down to blue-black of his well-defined jaw and full-formed mouth that reflected—surely as much as her own expression did—the state of his being. A sense of unreality washed over her, leaving her weak and suspending her breath in her throat. His features seemed as familiar to her as her best friend's, although she had never actually spoken to him until this afternoon.

'I——' she breathed fully for the first time in minutes, 'it—doesn't matter.' She sought desperately for a subject to neutralise the weirdness numbing her mind. 'What brought you to Rock Island—your brother's absence? The end of term can't be an easy time for a college professor to——'

'I've been here since summer,' he interrupted her babbling, mercifully taking his eyes from her as he settled into the chair opposite and lifted his glass to his mouth.

Sally stared uncomprehendingly. 'You mean you've—left university?'

He crossed one long leg over the other and she noticed for the first time that his feet were clad incongruously in soft brown leather slippers. There was no valid reason why Lyle Hemming shouldn't be wearing cosily domestic slippers, she reminded herself vaguely, but they just didn't fit into her

image of him as super-rake. Her eyes came up to
his face when he spoke again.

'A temporary leave of absence,' he said casually.
'There's a project I've been working on for some
time, and I'm at the stage now when I need the
isolation Rock Island provides.'

Sally's gaze sharpened. A doctoral thesis?—no,
he was already a Doctor of English Studies. A
scholarly work on one of history's great writers?

'I'm working on a novel,' he explained, proving
his point about her transparent expression. 'Until
John and Lorna left I managed to get quite a lot
done, but of course now——' He sighed regretfully,
and Sally immediately bristled.

'If you mean that my presence here will take you
from your work, please don't worry,' she said
stiffly. 'I'll be leaving as soon as I can get trans-
portation.'

'Your presence doesn't enter into it,' he retorted,
seeming surprised at the idea. 'Running a lighthouse is pretty well a twenty-four-hour operation,
and it's not the easiest thing in the world to write a
book when readings have to be recorded at set
times and reports on weather conditions have to
be sent at regular intervals. Your presence won't
affect that.'

Silently, Sally mulled over what he had just said
in a voice that laid no blame at her door yet which
made her feel guilty nonetheless.

'There must be something I can do to help while
I'm here,' she suggested spiritedly. She was a university graduate, presumably intelligent enough to
record data registered on automated machines. The
flight of fancy that had her manning, unaided, a

strategically placed lighthouse was brought to a
deflating halt by the Professor's eager acceptance
of her help in another area.

'Well, yes, there's a lot you can do around the
place to help out. If you can handle the meals and
generally take care of the housekeeper chores, I
can split my time between the book and the lighthouse operation.'

Animation faded from Sally's eyes as the import
of his words sank in. She was to take the traditional
role of homemaker while he did all the exciting
things. Lack of enthusiasm was evident in the cool
tone of her voice.

'Housekeeping isn't exactly my thing,' she
quoted his earlier words about cooking, and that
reminder was enough to set her stomach juices,
long deprived of sustenance, into motion. 'Isn't
dinner going to be ruined if we don't eat soon?'
she deviated from the subject of their conversation.

'It's a casserole Lorna left in the freezer,' he responded, though he rose glass in hand to look
quizzically down at her, 'so it won't spoil, but I
guess you're ready to eat something by now.'

The understatement of the year, she decided
when she rose dizzily to her feet, the light wine
having attacked her control centres. 'Yes, I—believe I could manage a bite or two. It's a long time
since I ate breakfast in the city.'

'Even longer till you eat your next breakfast
there,' he said with a hint of grimness.

Feeling chilled suddenly despite the fired warmth
of the room, Sally shivered and looked up into his
frowning face. 'The weather can't have got that

bad in such a short time,' she asserted with less confidence than she was feeling.

'No? Come and look.' His fingers curving round her elbow, their incisive force palpable even through the thickness of her sweater, he half dragged her to the windows and thrust aside the beige floral drapes. 'Any minute now,' he indicated the wisping curls of vapour undulating towards the light cast out by the double-glazed panes, 'the fog detector's going to sound its warning.'

As if his words were certain prophecy, a loud, unearthly wail from outside made Sally jump and press nervously close to the human form beside her. Every nerve in her body seemed janglingly aware of the deep bellow that filled the room and seemed to make its walls shake in reverberation. It was like a disembodied call from the grave, shattering her emotional patterns so that she clung, unaware, to the hard bodied comfort of the man beside her.

'It's all right,' he soothed, his sensitively shaped hand coming up to press her head to the hollow of his shoulder, his other arm encircling her waist protectively. 'You'll get used to it.'

The blast came again, only mildly muffled because of her ear being solidly attached to the scratchy wool of his sweater, and Sally trembled in the circle of his arms. But when the mournful wail at last faded away, another sound forced its way into her recognition. Lyle Hemming's heart, its beat strong and regular, thrummed against her ear and into her head, striking a different kind of chaos into her muddled thinking. A giggle of hysteria rose like a bubble to her throat. What wouldn't any one of his lovelorn students give to be in her position right now? The arms holding her were unbelievably gentle, the body she pressed herself against as virile and fit as they had dreamed of.

She sensed the downward tilt of his head and raised her own to meet it, feeling the snag of her hair on the rough fibres of his sweater, ignoring the third blast of the fog alert as a greater tumult engulfed her. Her eyes dropped to the firm outline of his lips, and there was an inevitability about the way his head dropped further and his mouth touched tentatively on hers.

She had kissed, and been kissed, many times before, but never like this. Never ever with this sweet rush of longing that made her legs tremble weakly under her when the first hesitant touch developed slowly, insistently, into an enveloping pleasure that encompassed the whole of her. Her lips parted in mindless acceptance of the experienced sensuality in his, her knuckles whitening as her fingers tightened convulsively on the textured wool of his sweater. Time slowed, then sped, marked off finally into some kind of rhythm by the guttural groans of the lighthouse.

'Let's go eat,' he said abruptly into her ear, pushing her from him with a force that left her blinking dazedly. Her dimmed wits told her he was rejecting her in no uncertain terms, and she groped numbly for a reason. He had been stirred in the same way as she had, every instinct told her that. But——

Not knowing what else to do, she followed his long stride into the kitchen and found him bent over the white enamelled stove, extracting the dish that had been titillating Sally's taste buds for what seemed hours. As he dished it up on the plates he had warmed by the stove and transported it to the table close by, it seemed as if nothing untoward had taken place between them. And it hadn't—for him, she realised with shocking bleakness as she obeyed his faintly irritated gesture towards the seat opposite his own. Her reaction was obviously worlds apart from his. After all, she had never made a habit of being available for casual sex encounters as he had. Out of date her principles might be, but they were hers, gleaned from thoughtful contemplation of the lives closely connected to hers. Her parents were the least conventionally-minded people she knew, yet it was unthinkable for her, their daughter, to imagine them as ever being less than totally committed to each other. For a man like Lyle Hemming, that kind of dedication to a relationship would likely seem prosaic, dull in the extreme.

Almost without her volition, her hand lifted her fork and she attacked the rich beef stew with an enthusiasm that overlaid the strung-out state of her nerves. 'Mmm, this is really good,' she appreciated aloud, picking up the glass he had refilled with white wine and looking at him without guile over its rim as she sipped. 'Your sister-in-law is an excellent cook.'

'Lorna? Yes, I suppose she is.'

'Don't you ever feel a need for a wife to take care of everyday needs?' she asked with thoughtless freeness as the wine and stomach filling food did their work on her physical system.

'Were you thinking of filling that bill on the strength of a few kisses?' he countered drily, neglecting his fork in favour of the glass an inch from his fingers. Tossing back the remaining liquid, he lifted the bottle at the back of the table and held it towards her glass with a faint lift of his eyebrows. When she refused with a shake of her head, he tipped the bottle over his own glass and filled it almost to the rim. 'What happened in there,' he indicated the living room with a nod of his head as he lifted the glass to his mouth, 'shouldn't give you any false hopes of orange blossoms and happy-ever-after endings. I'm strictly the non-marrying kind.'

Sally stared at him in speechless ire for long moments before she spluttered, 'What kind you are doesn't interest me at all, Dr Hemming. If I ever think of marrying, it won't be to someone like you!'

'Good. The last thing I need on my hands right now is a starry-eyed female who expects something I'm not prepared—or able—to provide.'

'Don't worry, Professor,' she bit back sarcastically, 'you don't interest me in the least as worthwhile husband material. In fact, I despise your kind of male, the type who—who finds women falling like bowling pins over his charms.' Her appetite fled on the storm that filled her, and she pushed her plate away in its half-finished state.

To her surprise, he chose not to lash back at her in return, instead saying mildly, 'You should finish your dinner, it's a long time till morning. And I think if we're to spend the next few days alone on this heap of rock you should drop the formality. My given name is Lyle.'

Lyle! As if she could call him that, immersed as

she still was in the university milieu that made such
familiarity impossible. How often had she heard
her contemporaries there breathe that name with
more than a suggestion of awed delight. 'Lyle,' they
had repeated endlessly. 'Lyle—isn't it a fantastic
name? It's so strong, masculine—just like him
somehow.' As if his parents had been blessed with
a supernatural kind of foresight, knowing their son
would grow up to be every co-ed's dream of male
perfection! But not for her, Sally gave herself the
stringent reminder. More important to her than
male charms was a sense of humour, an understanding that made light of the worries that beset
her as a woman—as a person—in a rapidly chang-
ing world.

'Thank you,' she acknowledged stiltedly, 'but I
doubt if I'll be here long enough to get used to
that kind of informality. I was brought up to——'

'For God's sake,' he interrupted with an irritable
frown, 'we're surely far enough away from the
nursery to want to cling to age-old fallacies. For
instance,' he mocked, his eyes bright from the
sparkling wine he had imbibed, 'my mother used
to tell me to beware of women who knew their
way around the world.'

Sally knew the comment needed no answer, yet
she made one just the same. 'I needn't ask if you
followed her advice!' she said acidly. 'I imagine
you've played the field in your time.'

'Then your imagination presumes a lot—too
much,' he responded with a frown she was beginning to recognise, one his students must have been
familiar with. Far from intimidating Sally, however, it merely made her more conscious of her own

invulnerability to his abrasive personality.

'Imagination plays a large part in my working life,' she said lightly, her fingers tightening round the slender stem of her glass as she lifted it to her lips. 'I don't write fiction, but my kind of work requires a certain amount of imagination too. Not that you novelists don't need a double dose of that too,' she conceded, plying her fork again on the plate he had pushed back to her place, 'but it must be a whole lot easier to write about things that might have happened but never did. What's your theme?' she ended abruptly, watching his expression with the close concentration of a reporter.

'My—what?'

'The germ of your story, the meat of it.'

'I don't think I want to talk about that,' he said flatly, pushing back his chair and looking meaningfully at her plate. 'Have you finished? I'm afraid dessert will have to consist of canned pears without cream.'

'I don't usually eat dessert,' she told the untruth without blinking, sensing that he wouldn't have bothered himself about dessert if not for her presence.

'Coffee, then?'

'Please. Can I—see to these dishes?'

'If you like. I don't care for instant coffee myself, so I can give you a hand while it's perking.'

No protestations, as most of her girl friends would have made, about leaving the dishes in the sink, they would be done later, Sally mused with a wry inward smile as she collected their plates and carried them to the sink under the window. She found a plastic bottle of washing liquid in the cupboard underneath and had run a sinkful of hot soapy water before Lyle picked up a cotton towel and took the first plate from the dishrack.

'Are you this neat in your Seattle apartment?' she asked facetiously as the second plate was extracted from the rack, still dripping suds.

'Yes,' he admitted truthfully. 'When you're brought up on a lighthouse, you learn to be neat and shipshape at all times.'

'Oh.' Sally sank her hands into the suds and recalled the spartan neatness of her bedroom and, in fact, every part of the house. It was a quality she had observed at the other lighthouses she had visited, particularly in the tower itself. 'May I come with you next time you go over to the lighthouse?' she asked casually, not really expecting a refusal, so his quick frown of displeasure surprised her.

'Maybe tomorrow,' he tossed back noncommittally. 'You wouldn't see much when I make the evening recordings.'

'How often do you make them?'

'Eight times a day—which also covers the night hours, of course.'

'You mean you have to get up in the middle of the night?'

He smiled drily at her astonished green gaze. 'I have an alarm clock that would waken the dead.'

'But you can't get more than a few hours' rest at any one time!' she exclaimed her concern, her hands lying idly in the soapy water as she twisted her head to look at him.

'It's not something I'd care to do for any length of time,' he admitted, 'but I can live with it until my brother gets back.'

'And when will that be?'

He shrugged. 'The boy's out of danger now, so they'll get back as soon as weather permits. As you know,' his mouth tightened to express his displeasure at her presence on Rock Island, 'that can't be for at least a week. Are you intending to leave those things to soak indefinitely, or can we get this job cleared away?' he ended impatiently.

Her cheeks burning at his abrupt manner, Sally groped for the square casserole dish and scrubbed feverishly at it with a nylon scraper. If she read the signs correctly, now wasn't the time to suggest that he take the time to teach her the rudiments of climate recording. And at this moment, she reflected sourly, she didn't really give a damn about his interrupted sleep. Being stranded on Rock Island was no more palatable to her than her presence there was to him. Any other human being would have been glad of company on the isolated outpost, but not Lyle Hemming. Was she such a poisonous personality that he found her company obnoxious?

She felt his eyes on her, perhaps in surprise, when she rinsed the casserole dish and dropped it violently on to the waiting dish drainer. Ignoring him, she emptied the red plastic bowl and rinsed it, then the sink.

'Coffee's ready,' he announced with uncaring detachment. 'You go on into the living room, and I'll bring it in.'

'You don't have to wait on me,' she snapped waspishly, drying her hands on the towel beside the sink and rolling the sleeves of her top down to wrist-length again. 'I'm quite capable of pulling my own weight here.'

'Fine,' he retorted equably, maddeningly so as his quiet tone made her own outburst seem shrewish in the extreme. 'We'll put that to the test tomorrow, but meantime——' His gesture towards the door was more than eloquent, and Sally walked towards it, saying no more.

Outwardly, at least. Inside, she was burning with an ire she didn't fully understand herself. The Professor was treating her as a nuisance, a necessary inconvenience in the order of his solitary life. He had been far more true to character, she cogitated silently as she stood staring down into the orange centre of the fire, when he had been making love to her there by the window. That had been the true Lyle Hemming, the darling of the co-ed set. Recalling his aloof attitude since those few moments of undistilled passion, she could only presume that His Romantic Highness had found her less than desirable as a passing fancy. And that, she told herself fiercely, was just how she liked it.

'I'll leave you to pour your own coffee,' he announced as he came into the room bearing a tray of percolator, china mugs, milk and sugar. 'I'll have mine when I get back.'

She heard him go soft-footed from the room and a pause in the hall while he donned lined jacket, presumably, and heavy rubber boots to replace his house slippers. Moved by curiosity, Sally moved to the window and watched the receding progress of a bobbing flashlight. When it was no longer visible, she turned back restlessly into the room and went to pour herself coffee from the freshly brewed pot, taking her mug to the chair that she had apparently accepted as her own.

Already she felt a confinement in her limbs, a constriction that made her long for a brisk walk on grass-covered hills. What in the world did they do for exercise on a rocky island like this? The Professor still had the appearance of flat-stomached fitness, but then his was only a temporary sojourn. What must it be like for people, like his brother and sister-in-law, who spent year in and year out on the physical confinement of the island? She made a mental note to bring that aspect into her article on lighthouses.

That thought led to another, and she wondered curiously just what Lyle Hemming's book was about. He had seemed extra reluctant to talk about it, so maybe it was one of those sex-filled commercially acceptable novels that were reviewed scathingly, if at all. But no, she couldn't really imagine that the dedicated professor of English would spend his time on trifles. It would be a literary work, meaningful and dripping with significance. If anyone could write that kind of book, it would be a man who had spent many years of his life instilling a love of literature into the students under his tutelage.

She looked round at the uncurtained windows, shivering as the mournful lowing of the fog alert penetrated the cosy inside scene. It was an eerie sound which the keepers must, in time, become used to, but for a newcomer it was curiously unnerving. She hadn't realised how keenly she was listening for Lyle's return until she heard the outer door open and slam shut, the pause as he changed back again into house clothes, the overwhelmingly welcome sight of his cold-reddened lean cheeks as he came into the room.

'I'll pour you some coffee,' she said quickly, her heart still knocking crazily against her ribs, although the sporadic wailing of the fog alert faded to insignificance the moment she saw his well-knit figure in the doorway. 'Do you take cream and sugar?'

He seemed to pause before coming forward into the room. 'Just sugar—two,' he informed her, his long legs stretching appreciatively before the glowing red of the fire as he took the winged armchair opposite hers.

'Was everything all right?' she asked as she handed him the cup of dark liquid, still steaming despite the lapse of time.

'Yes.' His tone denoted surprise at the question as he accepted the mug from her. 'The only worry on nights like this is for the shipping coming through the Straits. It's a lot easier being a lighthouse keeper than a ship's captain when the weather's like this.'

Silence fell between them while he downed his coffee and then reached to pour himself more, evidently not expecting Sally to repeat doing the honours for him, giving undoubted proof that his upbringing on a lonely lighthouse had made him extremely self-sufficient. In that regard, she gave a dry inner smile, her eyes on the neat, long-fingered economy of his movements. The women in his life were a different matter entirely.

His eyes unexpectedly lifted to hers as she settled back in her chair, something in his mocking expression telling her that he had possibly been party to her thoughts. Embarrassed, she cast about in her mind for a subject to break the silence.

'Where do you do your writing?' she asked, her face slightly flushed. She had seen no evidence of typewriter and paper in the pin-neat rooms she had glimpsed so far, and organised he might be, but she couldn't imagine that he cleared everything away out of sight between his writing stints. 'In the tower?'

'If you've visited other light stations, you must know that the tower mainly has room for only the necessary equipment,' he returned with a slight edge of sarcasm. 'No, I write in what used to be the assistant keeper's house, closer to the tower than this. I slept there, too, until John and Lorna left. They understand my need for privacy.'

And she didn't, his tone implied. 'Why couldn't you have stayed there?' she asked, her voice considerably cooler. If he imagined for one minute that there would be a repetition of that scene before dinner to distract, he was very much mistaken. Casual encounters of the sexual kind weren't her thing.

'Because it's more important to keep this house warmed and occupied than the smaller one,' he explained a shade irritably. 'Besides, the kitchen facilities are here. The assistant was always a single man, and he ate his meals here with the family.' His dark brows met in a frown she was rapidly becoming familiar with. 'I realise you have to ask questions for the sake of the article you're doing, but I'd prefer not to be mentioned in it myself. As I've said, privacy means a lot to me, and while I'll do my best to answer any questions you have about Rock Island and the lighthouse operation, my own work is strictly off limits.'

So that put her neatly in her place, Sally reflected with a dry touch of humour. That he apparently found it necessary to remind her of professional etiquette sat very differently with her, however.

'I think your privacy is quite safe, Dr Hemming,' she rejoined sarcastically, shuddering in a realistic way as the fog warning intruded again into her consciousness. 'Even if I brought you into the article in detail, I doubt if you'd find yourself overwhelmed by visitors anxious to explore the literary gems you're cooking up here.'

She felt a momentary pang of shame when dark colour rose to his face, but immediately defended her statement by telling herself inwardly that he had been less than welcoming since her arrival, making it clear that he considered her a necessary inconvenience because of his family's agreement to her visit.

'Gems or not,' he bit back abruptly, 'I've no wish to make my efforts public right now. What I'm working on is something of a deviation for me, and I've no idea yet as to how it's going to be accepted—if at all. As a writer yourself, you should understand that.'

'Oh, I do, Dr Hemming,' she agreed thoughtfully, 'indeed I do!'

So he *was* trying his hand at something she regarded as literacy prostitution! A work with commercial but very little other merit. Somehow the idea was painful to her, but she cloaked that feeling as she glanced at her watch and saw that it was a little after nine. While she hadn't seen her bed at that early hour since childhood, she felt an

overwhelming need to get away from Lyle
Hemming's presence, in search of the same privacy
he valued so highly.

'If you'll excuse me,' she said politely, rising to
her feet and going to the door, 'it's been a long
day for me and I'd like to write my notes up before
I go to bed.'

He rose just after her, his eyes mildly curious as
they rested on hers. 'You'll find it more comfortable to make any notes you might have down here
where it's warm. I should tell you that the bedrooms can get pretty chilly with the doors closed.
This is a convection type fireplace that depends on
openness for its efficiency, so I advise you to leave
your bedroom door open at all times.'

In a pig's eye, Sally told herself as she made her
way up the narrow staircase after thanking him
briefly and saying her goodnight. There was no way
that, with the campus pin-up in the room opposite
hers, she was going to leave her sleeping person
open to his view, heat or no heat. Regardless of
the fact that he had evidently reversed his previous
thinking, à propos that little scene before dinner,
she wouldn't trust a man with his reputation an
inch. The minuscule bedroom did seem a mite cold
after the warmth in the living room, and she made
a mental note as she used the small bathroom to
brush her teeth that in future she would make a
point of leaving her door open during the day.

In the meantime, she found her room so cold
that her fingers grew too stiff to write after a few
minutes perched, pad in hand, on the edge of the
bed. There wasn't that much to write yet anyway,
she salved her conscience as she salvaged her

nightdress from the round canvas bag containing her belongings. It hadn't been designed for arctic conditions, she regretted as she stripped to the skin and slid its pale green nylon folds over her head. But the thickly padded quilt covering the twin-sized bed promised comforting warmth, and she slid between sheets that were a practical flannelette and conveyed cosiness in their napped cotton.

Covers drawn up to her chin, she contemplated the white-painted ceiling as she recalled the events of the day. Not the least of the shocks to her system had been provided by her perilous boat journey to this, the remotest of the lighthouses she had visited. It was a whole new spectrum, she mused. The other light stations she had made part of her article had been remote but accessible, joined as they were to land. Rock Island was completely different, not only in its island isolation, but in the fact that she had found, not the keepers she had been expecting, but Lyle Hemming, a man she would have said was as far removed from an isolated light station as the moon was from earth.

Such a background was completely alien to her preconceived ideas about him. If she had been asked, she would have conjectured that he was the product of an affluent urban family, his career taking a preordained course. But she hadn't, and was never likely to be, asked about her opinion of him as a person. Until that afternoon she had never even spoken to him. He had been a figure only on the periphery of her consciousness. She reached from under the covers and snapped off the rosy glow of the bedside lamp.

So why had she felt, for those few minutes in his

arms, as if she had always known him, always known that one day she would end up there in his arms?

CHAPTER THREE

SALLY wasn't sure at first how long she had been asleep. It was still dark beyond the small window-pane when she woke from dreams punctuated by the groans of the fog alert. She groped for the bed-lamp switch and peered owlishly at her watch, taking in that the hands pointed to three-fifteen.

With that knowledge came the awareness that the room was deathly cold, her every sinew tensed against it despite the heavy layer of bedcovers. Her reluctant host hadn't been fooling about leaving her door open to the circulation of heat from the downstairs fire! For a moment she sat up and hugged her knees under the covers, which slid from her shoulders and instantly made mockery of the insulating value of her nylon nightdress.

She threw back the covers with an irritated ex-clamation, deciding as she padded barefoot to the door that modesty was an unnecessary luxury in a situation like this. Her hand had curved round the handle when the fog alert jangled against her nerve endings and she threw the door open with more vehemence than was strictly necessary. What had possessed her to take on this lighthouse assign-ment? It had seemed a romantic kind of life to her unaware senses at one time, those senses having been swamped by the literature she had delved into on the history of lighthouses before embarking on the task. It wasn't until now that she realised where the true heroism had lain in the pioneer days of lighthouse keeping. It wasn't the ever-present possibility of having to rescue shipwrecked mariners, it was the possession of a physical constitution that would enable them to withstand the horrific discomforts of a light station!

Her head lifted and her eyes closed in ecstasy as a flow of warm air engulfed her when she took a step into the narrow hallway. Goosebumps flared along the surface of her skin, then disappeared as the warm air smoothed them out. Her thoughts ran on an ironic line. Everything in life was relative, it seemed, the basic necessities being taken for granted by most people for most of the time.

She pulled her head abruptly down and to the side, her eyes flying open as she heard the sound of the downstairs door being closed quietly, stealthily. Her breath became suspended in her throat when, after a pause, steps came softly to her eardrums, creaking on the stairboards as they ascended higher and higher. Petrified, she watched the dark shape of a man appear through the short stretch of banister, his shadow thrown forward in grotesque relief on the wall at the head of the stairs.

A gasp escaped her half paralysed throat and the eerie light swung round and flashed on her, blinding her. Her hands automatically came up to shield her eyes, staying there even when she heard Lyle's familiar voice utter a muffled oath.

'What the hell——?' he questioned, mercifully lowering the flashlight to waist height as he came up to Sally's shaking figure. 'What's wrong?'

'I—I thought—somebody was—breaking in,' she stammered, her eyes reaching beyond the light to his shadowed face.

'Breaking in?' he echoed blankly, and then he gave a short laugh. 'That's one worry we don't have on Rock Island. Somehow the criminal element in our society draws the line at risking landing a boat at night on rocks as perilous as these.'

It had been a foolish assumption, she agreed as her brain came back into full working order, but he didn't have to point that out quite so forcefully. 'Like most people roused from sleep,' she disdained, rising to the five foot six that was still considerably under his height, 'I was a little disorientated for a while.'

'What roused you? Me?'

'I don't know,' she responded irritably, her hands finally dropping from her eyes to cross surreptitiously in front of her, one arm shielding her breasts from his male view in belated recognition that her nightdress must be almost transparent in the strong light trained on it. 'This isn't the most peaceful spot on earth, is it? That damn foghorn wails like a banshee all the time.'

'Is that what you thought I was?' he asked, amused. 'I can assure you, Miss Brown, that we don't run to ghosts any more than we do to thieves that pounce in the night.' His voice hardened. 'As the saying goes, if you can't stand the heat why don't you stay out of the kitchen? You might be better off with a nice safe husband in the suburbs instead of racketing around the country getting copy for articles that won't live longer than the time it takes to read them.'

Sally drew a swift, indignant breath. 'I suppose you think your kind of cheap book will last longer than the time it takes to read it?' she flared.

'Cheap? What are you talking about?' She trembled, even in the dim upglow of the flashlight, at the instant hardness that outlined his face like the implacable rocks surrounding the island.

'The book you're writing,' she brazened, refusing to give in to the instinctive feeling that she was biting off considerably more than she could chew. 'How much do you expect to make from it, Dr Hemming?' she scorned, her eyes reflecting glitteringly against the light trained on them.

'Very little,' he responded after a momentary pause. 'Why should you think otherwise? No, you obviously do,' he persisted as she made a dismissing gesture with her shoulders. 'What makes you think I'm working on something that will be commercially valuable?'

It was ridiculous, Sally told herself, that she should be standing here in a narrow hallway on a desolate island discussing the commercial worth of the Professor's literary efforts. Nevertheless, she wasn't about to renege on her conviction that he had sold out to the cheap and titillating aspect of publishing.

'I thought,' she said, her voice thick with cynical sweetness, 'that you might be writing an exposé on the women you've bedded, if not wedded.'

His hard indrawn breath could have been of pain, but that wasn't likely, she knew. A man like him, choosing women like adornments for his flowered buttonhole, wouldn't give a damn for their pain as he crushed them underfoot when their usefulness ended. What he said next did nothing to alter that feeling.

'How did you guess?' he mocked, his voice gravel-hard. 'In fact, the last chapter hasn't been written yet. How would you like to take a starring role in that?' His face was in shadow, yet she felt the tawny warmth of his eyes flick down the length of her and come back to the arm she held protectively over her breasts. 'You're a little leaner than most of my women, but I think I could come to terms with that.'

Sally stepped back into the doorway of her bedroom as he stepped purposefully towards her, her hands dropping from their protective position to grasp the doorknob in her agitated fingers. The full enormity of her circumstances sent crashing waves of awareness into her as the Professor dropped the flashlight on the floor and lifted his long-fingered hands to her bare arms. He could force himself on her, he could reach the ultimate of raping her, and no one would know or care about his violation of a woman who, they would say, had left herself open to just such occurrences by the nature of her job.

'Don't!' she ejaculated sharply when his hands dropped and slid from her arms to her waist and rested there for a moment on her waist before moving up to span her ribcage.

'You didn't make any objections earlier tonight,' he stated with irrefutable logic as he moved his body in close alignment with hers, his muscled thighs tensing against hers, his fingers insinuating themselves under her chin to raise her panicked face to his in the dim light from the lamp. 'You're no virginal lamb being led to the slaughter, are you?'

The scream of denial was lost when his mouth
came down and cut off its articulation. Mutely, she
felt the hard pressure of his lips making her own
reluctant participants in the grotesque scene that
followed, where his mouth took bondage of hers
and his hands moved up over her ribs to encompass
the soft swell of her breasts.

She held herself stiff against him, her brain de-
nying the hard press of his body, the drowning
sensation that clamped her throat when his thumbs
found and circled the roused points of her breasts.
Her bare foot lifted, then subsided uselessly against
the thick fabric encasing his legs. The frightening
realisation of her own vulnerability came when she
felt herself lifted and carried without effort to the
bed she had left only minutes before.

His lean form pressed into her, making her
frighteningly aware of his maleness, his superiority
in terms of physical mastery. She tasted the fierce
heat of his mouth as it explored the soft, warm
recesses of hers, and the body she had prided herself on controlling turned sudden traitor on her.
Her mouth softened to the hardness in his, becoming receptive to the explicit demands that made
nonsense of scruples accumulated over the passage
of years. She didn't care that Lyle Hemming was
making nonsense of scruples she had held dear
from time immemorial. Now was devastatingly
now, her every unconscious need being brought to
an inevitable conclusion by a man she scarcely
knew. He was making her more conscious of her
femininity than any man had done before, her hips
lifting to the demand of his as he made love to the
unawakened centre of her being, and she felt

violated, yet unused, when he lifted his body away from her and said mockingly,

'The first of the last chapter, Miss Brown. There's lots of time to make it more interesting to commercial tastes.'

She lay inert as he rolled from her and stood beside the bed, his completely clothed appearance making her conscious of her own flimsy covering.

'Damn you!' she breathed, feeling safer when she had wriggled under the quilted bed-coverings, pulling them up to her neck.

'I was damned a long time ago,' he mocked from his shadowy stance over her, 'by a much more potent force than yours.'

For some reason, that statement sent a jangle of irritation through her exposed nerves, and she gritted through her teeth: 'Get out of here, and don't come back unless you want me to report your behaviour to the coastguard authorities!'

He gave a low, mirthless chuckle. 'How much credence do you think they'd place in the unsupported word of a female journalist? Your breed isn't exactly known for its chaste guarding of virtue—in fact, they'd find it hard to believe that a woman who hightails it across the country in search of newsprint has any innocence left to protect!' His shadow moved from across her, and he jeered softly from the doorway, 'Goodnight, Miss Brown. Pleasant dreams.'

Sally's head swivelled on the pillow, her eyes searching in the gloom for something to throw at his arrogant head, but there was only the bedside lamp, and even that outline was doused in stark darkness when Lyle Hemming picked up the flashlight and disappeared across the hall. Her eyes sparked their own light of fury as she lay fulminating in the darkness.

The insufferable conceit of the man! Not to mention the prejudice widely circulated about women reporters, one she had become inured to—almost. She hadn't expected someone as young and literate as Lyle Hemming to foster outdated preconceptions of hardbitten women journalists as depicted in ancient movies. The thought pained her in some obscure way, as if its acceptance diminished him in her eyes. Yet how could the confirmation of her long-held opinion of him diminish his stature to any extent? He had already been at the bottom of the morality stakes in her view long before she set foot on Rock Island.

Too wrought up to recapture sleep, she lay in seething quietness plotting the Professor's downfall. A vindictiveness she had been unaware of possessing took control of the being she had prided herself on, its cool impartiality. Revenge might not be sweet, as the saying promised, but it would be eminently satisfying.

She was realistic enough to know that any complaint on her part to the authorities would be met by the disbelief he had promised, so there must be another way, an area in which he was vulnerable. His morals were no better and no worse than any other man's in his position. Besides, she had no real concrete proof that he was a womaniser, and she was journalist enough to know that being sued for libel was no picnic. No, it had to be something else, something that was irrefutable fact, yet which he wouldn't want dragged into the light of day. It hit her then.

The dazzling perfection of her brain-child sent her wriggling ecstatically down between the covers. His book! He had been at pains to make sure that her lighthouse coverage should say nothing of his presence on the island, or of the work he was engaged on. It was perfect! All she had to do was discover the name he wrote under for his commercially-orientated opus, and then blow his cover sky high. The university authorities would hardly look kindly on his extra-curricular activity if it detracted from the university's credibility as a serious institute of learning, so Lyle Hemming would be sent to oblivion on skis greased liberally by herself.

Not questioning whether or not she was overreacting to purely personal circumstances, she drifted off into comfortable sleep as dawn sent pale fingers of light into the tiny bedroom.

She awoke from a dream of sailing with her father, a voyage that had been storm-tossed and then smoothly peaceful. Her eyes went round the unfamiliarity of her surroundings, the door opened wide to the passage beyond, the plainly crafted chest of drawers and the narrow door of the clothes closet.

Groping, she reached for her watch and peered at its unadorned face. Nine-thirty! Sitting up, she swung her legs over the bed's side and looked searchingly around her. Something was missing. As the raucous cawing of a gull screeched somewhere outside the window, she realised what was missing from the scenario. The husky bleating of the fog alert no longer disturbed the natural peace of the

light station, and she shot from the bed to pad
barefoot across to the window. The weather had
cleared, she sang exultantly inside herself, her
hands reaching for the brace of the wood frame,
she could go home and——

'Oh, no!' she whispered brokenly. Dense grey-
black clouds hung like a pall over the sullen anger
of the ocean, and even her inexperienced eye could
see that no one in his right senses would attempt a
landing at Rock Island in those conditions. She
hadn't realised how high her hopes had been until
something slumped inside her and left her feeling
bleak. Maybe Lyle Hemming had been right, and
she would be marooned here on this desolate pile
of rocks for a week or more.

Remembrance of the night's intrusion made her
shiver and tilt her head in a listening attitude. Not
a sound penetrated up the narrow staircase, and
she conjectured with relief that the Professor must
be tending his business at the tower. Leaving the
window, she scrabbled in her travel bag and
brought out fresh jeans and underwear, picking up
her thick yesterday's sweater to add to the pile as
she sought the privacy of the miniature bathroom.

Water for her shower ran hot until she cooled it
with the frigid cold tap, then, disdaining the strong-
smelling bar soap that had obviously been used to
lather her host's hard-knit body, soaped herself
with the lightly scented toiletry she had brought
with her. The cleansing spray afterwards did
nothing to alter the decision she had taken during
the night to expose Lyle Hemming as the literary
charlatan he was. More in possession of herself
than she had been then, dull though the daylight

might be, she rubbed herself dry and thought coolly
of her plan of campaign.

It shouldn't be an insurmountable problem to
get into the assistant keeper's house where the
Professor did his work. Even he had to sleep some
time, and she doubted he would take the precau-
tion of locking the door after his day's stint was
done. She might even, she mused, drawing on her
jeans, make notes of salient passages in the manuscript and incorporate them, with suitable sarcasm,
in her article. Already the form of that article was
taking place in her busy brain. 'Without doubt, the
English Professor has drawn fully from life—his
own life, that is, replete with details gained from
his numerous encounters with his opposite
gender.'

A stark note, inviting her coolly to help herself
to anything she might need, awaited her on the
square kitchen table. The note was couched in far
from intimate phraseology, apart from the flowing
signature of 'Lyle'. She would rather, she mused as
she set the note aside and delved into a box labelled
'Bread', that he had refrained from that suggestion
of friendly closeness between them. They were not
now, and would never be considered, friends. A
cobra would be preferable—at least that didn't
have arms that bound and hands that provoked
sensations best left to the marriage bed.

Her eyes widened and took on a glazed veneer
as she waited for the toast to pop up. Marriage
seemed alien to a creature like Lyle Hemming; bed,
yes. It wasn't hard to imagine the attraction women
felt for him, the certainty they must have that he
would provide every answer to their dreams of the

ideal mate. Even she—yes, if she was honest she
would admit it—even she had felt the pull of that
magnetism, the physical potency that overrode
every other consideration. For a short time, she
consoled herself, her hands consciously steady as
she spread butter and country-style jelly on her
toast and poured coffee from the half-filled percolator on the stove. On a more conscious level, he
was everything she despised in a man. Confident,
arrogant, sure of what he wanted and how to get
it.

Having eaten, she stacked her dishes in the red
bowl set inside the sink and paced restlessly
through the house. The glass doors she had noticed
the night before opened to the blazing fire were
now closed over its more subdued flame in the
living room and needed no attention. She wandered
over to the window and looked out at the lowering
greyness, her attention caught by a wisp of smoke
curling up from a point to her left. Her eyes followed the plume downwards to its square smoke-
stack and red-tiled roof showing above a depression in the rocks. It was hardly surprising that she
hadn't noticed it the day before, bewildered as she
had been to see Lyle, not John, Hemming turning
out to greet her.

Her eyes lingered on the red-tiled roof for long
moments, and then she turned and went out to the
hall where her winter jacket hung on the row of
pegs inside the front door. Claustrophobia, as per-
vasive as the cloud wisps that hung over the island,
crept insidiously over her and propelled her into
action, albeit a necessarily curtailed action. She let
herself out of the house and stepped off along the

entrance path and its pathetic tubs of greenery
bordering it. Lorna Hemming must be a supreme
optimist, she reflected wryly, to think that anything
worthwhile would flourish in a windswept spot like
this.

The green swathes she had taken for grass turned
out to be lichens and moss clinging to the rocky
terrain. It was like a carpet underfoot, and
provided charm in the intermingling shades of
green. Rosettes of leaves where flowers would later
blossom nestled closely to the inhospitable rock,
mingled with the lichen carpet that gave, then
sprang back to sturdy life under her footprints.

Like a siren's call, the tower beckoned her, forbidding yet comforting in its solid thrust of concrete and steel. Sally crossed by a wooden bridge
that spanned a moat-like encirclement round the
edifice, and found herself at the white painted steel
door of its entrance.

A quick glance over her shoulder showed that
only the main house was visible from where she
stood, and curiosity stretched her fingers towards
the ring clasp set into the door. She was surprised
at how easily it swung outwards, inviting her into
its shadowy, dim interior. She gave a last look
behind her, then stepped inside.

Light filtered down from the spiral stairs leading
up from the base area, which housed a con-
glomeration of machinery which interested her not
at all and led her eyes up to the floors above. Her
hand gripped the side rail as she went boldly up
the winding staircase, the small-paned window half
way up blinding her as she stared out from it to
the white-capped waves breaking on jagged-edged

rocks. Something of their wild spirit invaded her and she pressed up towards the next level, where a window on the far side of the tower illuminated a round room filled with clicking machinery. Walking to the middle of the room, she let her gaze travel round the collection of dials and switches in their bewildering array, reflecting that a person would have to possess the skills of an engineer to understand them. She mentally notched up a point or two in Lyle Hemming's favour. Obviously, their intricate precision posed no problem to his being able to take over the smooth running of a lighthouse at the drop of a hat.

She was bent over the jerking point of a weather gauge when a voice, seeming disembodied as it rang round the circular room, accosted her.

'Can I help you with something?'

Sally's breath was expelled in a series of sighs as she whirled round and recognised the intruder.

'Oh!' she breathed, inexplicably relieved to see Lyle Hemming's broadly competent figure outlined against the dim interior light. 'No, I—I just wanted to—to see what was up here.'

'I doubt if it's any different from the other lighthouses you've visited,' he said, his hand flicking to a switch that immediately flooded the area with blinding light. He came towards her, his hips narrowly smooth in tight-fitting jeans, the chest tapering up and out from them covered in a red and black plaid shirt that would more appropriately have dressed a lumberjack. 'Are you interested in the mechanics of lighthouse keeping?'

Sally's mouth felt inexplicably dry, and she ran a moistening tongue over her parched lips as she turned to stare blindly at the black pointed arrows that surely indicated some vital information. 'I—I like to research my background thoroughly,' she mustered finally, and felt an alien jet of gratification at his serious nod of approval.

'Good, that's important in your line of work. I'll try to be as concise as possible about what goes on here, but if you have any questions, feel free to ask them. Now, let's start off with this monster here.'

He moved to the first machine in the roundel and began a crash course in the technical duties of a lighthouse keeper that left her breathless with admiration for the concise method of his delivery, bearing in upon her senses the knowledge that, as a teacher, he was without equal. The precise, logical sequence of his words, tempered with a wry humour, made her feel like an expert by the time the last machine in the circle had had its function explained to her.

'It's not an intellectually demanding job,' he disparaged, 'it's more a question of regularity and application. A person has to have a certain quality of character to run a light station efficiently.' A quality, his tone seemed to imply, he didn't possess himself.

'I'd have liked to meet your brother,' Sally said without thinking, and Lyle straightened from the instrument he had been gauging, giving her an abstracted sideways glance before entering some figures on a ledger sheet beside him.

'You probably will,' he said, vaguely inattentive. 'Though it won't be a protracted meeting. As he arrives, you'll leave on the same boat. As you've no doubt noticed, the rocks surrounding the island aren't conducive to lengthy stays.' And then his eyes lost their abstraction and focused mockingly on her. 'What's the matter, Miss Brown? Were you hoping for a lengthier acquaintance with a more worthy member of the family than me? I can assure you that John's knowledge of the operation may be of longer duration, but I'm quite competent.'

'I don't doubt it for a minute,' Sally responded on a dry note, moving to her left and scanning a black-figured dial without seeing it. 'If there's one quality I've noticed about you, Dr Hemming, it's your competency.'

As if her use of his title had brought into sharp focus for him, too, his expert way of coping with the co-eds who fell like ninepins under his charm, he pivoted on one foot and stared hard at her.

'You say that as if there's something wrong in turning average English grades into work that shows promise,' he said coldly, and Sally knew that the wave of mild guilt that flowed through her was more than justified. Lyle Hemming's students were renowned for their widened appreciation of English language and literature, whatever the cause of their accelerated interest. The thought came to her fleetingly that he didn't care about methods, only their results. If they meant using the blind adoration of the students under his care to foster a greater understanding of their subject, it didn't matter to him.

'How many published writers have you produced, Professor?' she jeered in a venomous tone she hardly recognised as her own, and she wasn't prepared for the fury of his reaction.

'Writers? Maybe none.' His tawny eyes flailed

the false bravado in hers. 'But I've produced men
and women who use the creative part of their imagination in daily living. Men who find value in
the rituals of making their living, women who appreciate the potential of their offspring as well as
their own aspirations. Dr Jeffreys is a master of his
subject, but he sure as hell failed when he produced
a woman as narrow in her views as you are.'

'I'm not narrow in my views!' she flared. How
could she be, with parents who lived in a manner
that others would construe as unconventional?
They had never constricted her in any conventional
way, and Sally resented his implication that she
was anything less than a fully rounded person.
True, their lives might be considered prosaic in a
world that regarded marital fidelity as quaint in
their artistic sphere, but did that necessarily mean
that they were restricted in their views? 'A sense of
morality begins long before university,' she inserted
into the silence that enveloped them apart from
the raucous cawing of a gull outside the tower.

'What kind of morality are we talking about?'
he questioned, for all the world as if they were
comfortably installed in the academic surroundings
which would make such a discussion plausible, instead of in a rounded tower set on the edge of
nowhere. The machine she leaned against was
making, she was certain, a permanent ridge against
her hip. But the discussion was alive in a way Dr
Jeffrey's dissertations had never been, and Sally
spared a fleeting stab of envy for the students
whose minds had been stimulated by a colourful
character named Lyle Hemming. 'There's the morality of caring for others less fortunate, or the

morality of preserving the environment for future generations, or——'

'Morality to me,' Sally interposed forcefully, 'is the commitment two people make to one another to be faithful, loyal, true. Everything else stems from that.'

'Don't you think your viewpoint is limited to personal commitment?' he posed, then his feet moved restlessly round the confined area of the tower, for all the world as if he was pacing the rostrum in a tiered classroom. 'In the world of today we face—each and every one of us—the prospect of annihilation from a variety of explosives designed expressly for the purpose. In that context, personal commitments are a minor consideration. I'd rather have heard you mention the horrendous impact chemical effluents were making on the ecology, or the long-reaching effects of nuclear warfare. Those are two of the most pressing problems young people should be coming to grips with today.'

'There's not a lot they can do about it, is there?' she asked, her tone sarcastic.

He shrugged. 'Individually, no. But if enough people make their concern known, something might come of it. Don't tell me you've never participated in a demonstration, or a sit-in?' he enquired mockingly, coming to a halt in front of her, hands thrust deep into the side pockets of his jeans.

'One or two,' she admitted cautiously, 'but very little was accomplished.'

He nodded thoughtfully but said nothing. Sally grew uncomfortable under his level stare, feeling

those tawny eyes dredging up every failing of
character from the deepest recesses of her being,
assessing them . . . assessing her as a person. Was
this the hypnotic effect he exerted on his students?
she wondered, her legs suddenly weakening under
her as if he was drawing her most vital resources
from her. A wry conviction winged through her.
Those women students who adored him must have
been subjected to this same kind of scrutiny and,
coupled with their appreciation of his faintly
melancholy good looks, wrought havoc in their
pounding hearts. Her own pulse was only too
aware, at this moment, of the attraction he exuded
to her every sense, stirring all that was feminine in
her. When he spoke, his voice evenly normal, she
started out of her mesmeric state as if he had
shouted.

'You might as well see the rest of the place now
you're here,' he gestured to the stairs spiralling still
farther up, and she followed him numbly to the far
side of the room, placing her feet automatically
where his had been on the open iron gridwork of
the staircase.

Under other circumstances, she would have been
far more personally and professionally interested
in the lifebeat of the light station. As it was, she
noted the huge reflectors half abstractedly, her eyes
going to the curtained circular windows surrounding this highest level of the lighthouse.

Noticing her glance in that direction, Lyle explained, 'These windows are kept curtained during
the day so that, from a distance, the tower is dis-
tinguishable as a separate unit, white apart from
the red spiral, which is invaluable in heavy snow

areas to distinguish it from the surrounding area.'

Telling herself that she preferred his precise explanations to the uncomfortable effect he had on her when he was expanding on a philosophical theme, Sally went first this time as they retraced their steps to the middle level, and from thence to the lowest point of the lighthouse and the breath-catching wind outside. She looked hopefully up at the scudding clouds. Maybe a wind that strong would blow them away and bring enough tranquillity to make a safe landing on Rock Island.

'Don't pin your hopes on an early rescue,' her host bent to say in her ear as if he had accurately read her thought. 'By nightfall the fog alert will be busy again.'

'How I hate it!' she shuddered, hunching her shoulders down into the sheepskin warmth of her jacket.

'My mother did too. It was the one aspect of lighthouse keeping she detested above everything else.'

Sally frowned and glanced back at him as he followed her across the soft springing moss. 'Yet she stayed here without complaining?'

His windblown chuckle had become faint by the time it reached her ears. 'Not without complaint, no.'

'Yet your father made her stay here, bring her family up here?'

His fingers were still busily buttoning the lined jacket he had picked up from the iron rail just inside the lighthouse. 'It was his life,' he said simply, drawing level with her and stopping to let his eyes roam over the rocky island, his dark hair whipped over his forehead by the wind. 'He didn't make her do anything. She accepted the hardships when she married him.'

'Just as your sister-in-law accepts your brother's way of life?'

'Yes. Although Lorna's used to it. Her father was a keeper, and she was brought up to the isolation, so it isn't a problem for her.'

'She must sometimes need the amenities of civilisation occasionally, though.'

'What?' His head bent towards her as they began walking again, the wind having whipped the words from her mouth and borne them mainly out to sea.

'Doesn't she need other people occasionally?' she repeated in a louder tone and saw his shoulders lift under his jacket in a shrug she was becoming familiar with.

'She seems contented enough, and they have a month off the island every year.'

'Who takes care of the station then?'

'There's a relief keeper on the mainland.'

Sally decided to give up on conversation at that point, difficult as it was against the gusty force of the wind. In any case, she realised, staring curiously at the building they had been walking towards, unless she was very much mistaken she was about to be taken into the lair where Lyle Hemming churned out his potboilers.

CHAPTER FOUR

HER first impression was of cosy warmth as Lyle held open the door of the assistant keeper's cottage and gestured her inside. The source of heat, she quickly identified, was a small black pot bellied stove set half-way along one wall of what was virtually a one room cabin. Two worn armchairs were set on either side of it, and a divan bed filled the larger part of the opposite wall. Under the small-paned window that looked out on to the light tower and the grey sullenness of sea beyond was a table loaded to capacity by a grey-black typewriter and manuscript pages scattered haphazardly across its surface. The untidiness there belied the spartan neatness in the rest of the room, the divan bed smooth under a heavy tapestry cover, the rugs dotted here and there on the polished wood floor without a trace of dust or lint on them.

'Can I offer you some coffee?' Lyle asked hospitably, shrugging his jacket from his broad shoulders and hanging it casually on a hook inside the door. Sally responded to his silent gesture and took off her own jacket, watching as he hung it neatly beside his.

'I thought the main house was the source of sustenance,' she remarked as she went farther into the cosily set up room.

'It's not always convenient to run across there every time I need a cup of black coffee,' he said

dryly, picking up a brass kettle from the brick surrounding the stove and shaking it with his head on
one side, listening. 'Good, there's enough water
here for a couple of cups.'

Sally walked over nearer the table, but all she
could discern was a blur of typescript. Not much
chance of gleaning information on his work there,
especially since the Professor would be in the room
with her at all times. She swung away from the
work table and came back to where he was busying
himself with china mugs and a jar of instant
coffee.

'I hope you can drink it black,' he said across
his shoulder. 'I'm not equipped to handle lady visitors.'

'Is it only women who drink cream in their
coffee?' she took him up immediately, and he
grimaced as he pulled open the tiny door of the
stove and threw more wood on to the glowing
embers from a neatly stacked pile beside the stove.

'I asked for that one, didn't I? I'm not usually
that chauvinistic, but it's true in my experience that
more men than women take their coffee black.
However, I haven't taken a census on it, so don't
quote me.'

A flush that had nothing to do with the heat
from the stove spread uncomfortably to her face.
By using that faintly mocking tone of his, he had
very efficiently and expertly put her down, intending her to feel her female objection was small and
petty.

'I'll take mine black,' she said tartly, and sat
down in one of the worn armchairs, its grooved
impressions making it obvious that she had taken

his chair. From it, he could see the tower looming eerily not far distant, keep his eye on the light, though in this automated age it was likely that, if one light failed, an emergency system would come into force immediately. Breaking the silence that had come between them, Sally asked him about it and he turned from his contemplation of the kettle, which was just beginning to show steam.

'It's happened once or twice,' he nodded, pushing his hands into his pockets, drawing her attention to the smooth line of his hips, the taut muscles of his thighs. How many women had known those strongly shaped thighs intimately? She could still feel their hard outlines pressed to hers in the semi-darkness last night in her bed . . . and you couldn't get much more intimate than in a bed! The colour in her cheeks deepened as, confused suddenly, she looked up and found his eyes trained on hers as he spoke. She realised she hadn't heard a thing he had said.

'. . . but that's just one of the hazards in a job like this. John knows what to do when an emergency comes along, although it's never happened that both systems have failed at the same time.'

'Wh-what would happen if they did?'

He gave his inimical shrug. 'Then there'd be a lot of very unhappy seamen out there in the channel.'

'Aren't most ships equipped with radar these days?' she gathered her scattered wits to ask.

'It's been known for radar to be off course at times if the weather's bad. Anyway, a lot of older sea captains prefer to rely on the lights.'

Steam streamed past his elbow and he turned to

take the kettle from the stove and pour bubbling water into their cups. He set hers on the hearth beside her chair, remarking, 'It's too hot to drink yet, better leave it for a while.'

An odd pang shot through Sally as she watched him straighten up and carry his own cup to the chair opposite, placing it beside him on the hearth before settling back in his chair, crossing his long legs over each other and looking disconcertingly across at her. The advantage, Sally realised belatedly, was his. His back was to the light from the windows, while her face took the full force of the daylight, obscured as it might be.

'So ... tell me about yourself, Sally Brown. What made you take up the job of reporting on other people's lives? Wasn't your own interesting enough?'

She blinked across at his shadowed face. No one else had ever asked her about her work in that particular way; they had either been over-enthusiastic about its glamour, or snidely knowing about what they imagined was her life of debauchery plunged eagerly into with the prominent people she interviewed for the magazine. She gave an uncomfortable laugh.

'Did all the greats in magazine writing take to it because they were bored in a personal way?' she parried. 'Or did they, like me, feel that their mission in life was to inform people about subjects and people they'd never otherwise come to know? To widen their outlook, and maybe bring understanding and tolerance to those who hold different views from their own?'

'Is that Dr Jeffreys speaking, or Sally Brown?'

he enquired sardonically.

'It probably has roots in Dr Jeffreys, but the main philosophy is my own,' she came back immediately, resenting his implication that she was devoid of her own personal convictions, that they had to be supplied by others. 'What's wrong, *Dr* Hemming,' she stressed sarcastically, 'does it distress you that Professor Jeffreys produced at least one writer, while you haven't been able to come up with one creatively viable student?'

'Distress me?' Lyle bent without uncrossing his knees to pick up his coffee and sip tentatively at it. 'No, I don't think so. I just seem to detect another kind of quality he's imparted to you. One that makes no room for human frailties, that life is cut and dried without respect for individual differences. He lives in the twentieth century, yet his mind still yearns towards the romantic poets of the sixteenth and seventeenth centuries. For all practical purposes he's a washout.'

'He is not!' she threw back with a vehemence that surprised herself. 'Oh, he might not go along with the looser morals of today, but he's a fantastic teacher. He made Virgil, Plato, Shelley——' she waved an encompassing hand, 'Shakespeare, come alive for me.'

" 'In the golden light'ning
    Of the sunken sun
    O'er which clouds are bright'ning,
    Thou dost float and run,
  Like an unbodied joy whose race is just
        begun," '

he quoted softly, the hard edge disappearing from his voice to endow it with a liquid eloquence that left her strangely weak as it flowed smoothly over her. How had Lyle Hemming known that particular quotation, one that wasn't all that well known?

'How did you——?' she queried with raised brows.

'How did I know that Dr Jeffreys uses Shelley in his curriculum?' Lyle said with a wry smile. 'Because, believe it or not, he was my teacher at university. He filled me with the same kind of romantic unreality as he obviously fed to you.'

'But you've learned better in the years between,' Sally rejoined, not so much with a question as the statement that she accepted his hardened philosophy that life was far removed from the unthinking acceptance of Dr Jeffreys' dictums.

'I've learned that life doesn't always fulfil that idealistic promise,' he said drily before applying himself to the remainder of his coffee. 'Life, that is, as Dr Jeffreys sees it.'

'Surely we bring disillusionment on ourselves?' Sally posed, not entirely sure of her own answer to that question. 'You can't blame your English professor for shortcomings in your own life.'

'No,' he agreed with a resignation that seemed untypical of his kind of man. 'I don't blame him for the shortcomings in my own life, but I'd have appreciated a more realistic assessment of what might go wrong in the idealistic world he painted for me and all the students under his care.'

'I think I know what you mean,' Sally said thoughtfully, her eyes abstracted as she reached for her cooled coffee and swallowed its throat-tingling pungency. 'It's important to appreciate the past,' she ventured carefully, 'but you should be able to apply that knowledge to the problems of today.'

'Exactly.'

His enthusiastic approval sent a warm thrill through her, and for a moment she was back in the classroom where warm sun streamed through long arched windows and dust motes danced in its yellow glow. With that vision came the remembrance of Dr Jeffreys on the podium, his silvery mane streaked to brilliance by that same sun. Had she been disloyal in tacitly agreeing with Lyle Hemming? Her aged professor had been dear, sweet, lovably out of this world in his immersion in a philosophy that had no connection with modern thinking. Yet he had touched chords of sympathy in herself and many of the students who heard him. He believed in an old-fashioned chivalry, a dedication to honesty in human relationships that made mockery of today's morality.

'Was he wrong to make a virtue of—virtue?' she asked, questioning herself although Lyle Hemming answered her thought.

'Probably not,' he said as he rose jerkily to his feet and looked down at her. 'But it might have been better if he'd injected a little realism into his lectures.' His long legs propelled him to the paper-strewn desk, and he stared down at the half-typed page in the typewriter. 'Look, if you don't mind I'd like to get on with some work now.'

The introverted dreaminess in her eyes faded abruptly, and she rose to her feet. 'Of course,' she said shortly, walking to the door and taking her jacket from the peg beside his. She felt inordinately hurt by his abrupt reversal from philosophical

professor to writer-in-action, but nothing of her
inner turmoil showed, she hoped, as she looked
back, her hand on the round doorknob. 'What
about lunch?'

He waved a dismissing hand. 'Fix something for
yourself,' he said almost irritably, looking up when
she still hesitated at the door. 'I don't normally eat
at noon, even Lorna has accepted that mad quirk
in my nature.'

'As you please.' Sally went out, closing the door
firmly behind her though her nerves felt bruised
somehow as she went across the cushiony lichens
to the main house. What was wrong with him? For
that matter, what was wrong with her? So, he didn't
want to eat with her, be close in any way to her
unwelcome presence on Rock Island. Why should
she care about Lyle Hemming's chameleon-like
nature, as warmly human as any man's one minute
and frigidly rejecting the next?

But it did matter, she discovered as she busied
herself making a man-sized lunch of ham between
thick wedges of bread, regretting the absence of
salad vegetables to round out the meal. She made
instant coffee and carried her lunch into the sitting
room, deliberately choosing the fireside chair that
kept her back to the window. Sight of the assistant
keeper's cottage with its plume of grey smoke indicating possession was a reminder she could happily
do without.

Yet the man she sought to shut out from her
consciousness was as vividly alive as if he sat
opposite her. She lifted the thick sandwich to her
lips and lowered it hurriedly again, her eyes drawn
to the barely visible red glow behind the glass doors

of the fire. Setting her plate aside, she went down on her knees and opened the doors, glancing round in search of kindling when she saw that logs, split though they might be, would never catch alight in that faint redness. The orderly pile of logs lodged into a bricked recess beside the fire offered nothing in the way of kindling, and she got up and wandered into the kitchen, not knowing what she was looking for until her eye fell on a sharp-bladed axe propped inside the store cupboard.

Carrying it by its stout handle, she took it into the living room and set a rounded log on the tiled surround to the fireplace. Her first tentative stroke made no impression on the wood that looked so dry and splintery—fir, she guessed, from its roughly serrated bark—and she raised the unwieldy axe higher over her shoulder, poising it there for a steadying moment before starting it on its downward way.

'What the hell do you think you're doing?'

The axe lost momentum and wavered before continuing on its descent, missing its mark and curving inwards so that the sharp blade sliced between her thumb and forefinger, drawing an immediate gush of deep red that spread over and stained the log's yellow interior.

'Ouch!' Sally glared over her shoulder at Lyle Hemming in the doorway, and said furiously, 'What the hell do you think *you're* doing, frightening me to death like that!'

She saw him start towards her, and she turned back to stare in sickened horror at the blood flowing from her flesh to the log.

'Did you——? Oh, my God!' He sounded more

disgusted than alarmed as he knelt quickly beside her and prised the axe handle from her fingers, which seemed to have frozen to it. Next, he touched her injured hand at the wrist, bringing it up closer to his hard eyed scrutiny. 'You're lucky,' he grunted, bending her arm so that her hand remained upright against her, 'it's just a surface wound. Wait here.'

What did he think she would do, she asked herself silently as he disappeared from her side—run out and swim to the mainland in search of a doctor? She looked at the gash between her fingers and felt faintness wash over her. Did surface wounds bleed that much? Swaying, she leaned back from the fireplace. The dying embers might be difficult to set alight with wood, but her hair was something else again.

'Okay, sit back against the chair and let me take a look at it.' The Professor's face swam dizzily in front of her eyes as he settled her square against the upholstery, his eyes gleaming with all the ferocity of a cougar's as he bent closer and stared into her face. 'Are you all right?'

'Oh, sure,' she joked weakly. 'My day wouldn't be complete without bloodshed. Didn't you know that doctors always used to bleed their patients to make them better?'

She was rambling inanely, she knew, but the sight of blood, particularly her own, always had that effect on her. Lyle seemed indifferent to her meanderings, concentrating his attention on cleaning and bandaging the wound he had called 'surface'. She drew in her breath on a sharp hiss when he poured something on it, and then it resumed its dull aching when he bound gauze in a tight swathe between her thumb and forefinger.

'Thank you,' she roused herself to say when he at last propped her hand upright against her again. 'Will I live, doctor?'

'You'll live,' he replied tersely, still on his knees beside her, 'though I'm not sure you deserve to. Why in hell didn't you call me to make up the fire?'

'You were busy, Professor.' She giggled weakly. 'Far be it from me to take the muse from his— musings.'

She heard his muffled oath and then his arms coming round, lifting her, carrying her up the narrow stairs to the upper floor.

'I can manage by myself,' she mustered dignity round her when she recognised the narrow confines of her room, and felt the bed yielding under her when he placed her on it with a decisive yet strangely gentle touchdown. The puffed quilt settled round her and was tucked securely at her sides.

His voice seemed to come from far away when he spoke. 'I'm not in the habit of attacking defenceless females, so relax and get some sleep. I won't be far away.'

She wanted to tell him how comforting that thought was, but when she opened her eyes moments—minutes?—later, he had gone. Struggling against the weakness that crept insidiously through every part of her, she sought desperately to recall something she had wanted to tell him, but it slid wraith-like from her grasp. . . .

'Sally? You awake?'

She blinked back to consciousness and stared uncomprehendingly round the half-dark room and then at the man whose breadth seemed to fill its narrow confines to capacity, shrinking it. Her eyes went over the checked shirt covering well-set shoulders, and full remembrance flooded over her.

'Wh-what time is it?' She struggled to one elbow under the downy weight of the quilt and peered at the dial on her right wrist, but her eyes were still too filled with sleep to discern the luminous figures.

'Almost six,' the Professor told her, his voice gentler than she had yet heard it. 'How's the hand?'

Sally stared at the neat white bandage bound round her wrist and thumb area, and only then felt the hot throb of the axe wound. 'Sore,' she grimaced, more with annoyance than pain. Now that the initial shock had worn off, it would be a pure hell of annoyance until it healed. Realising that might have sounded ungracious, she added, 'Thanks—for taking care of it for me.'

'As long as you've learned not to tackle things you've no experience with,' he told her with just a lightly censorious air. 'Supper's ready when you are.'

'Oh—thanks.' As on the evening before, tantalising food smells were drifting up to her room, reminding her that she hadn't eaten the sandwich she had prepared for lunch. This was how Lyle Hemming must feel every day at this time if he didn't eat during the day. 'I'm sorry.'

'For what?' He turned back from the door, dark brows raised quizzically.

'I really did mean to make dinner tonight, so that you could—get on with your work.'

'And probably slice a finger or two off with the paring knife,' he said sardonically. 'Thanks, but it uses up less of my time to throw a meal together than act as nurse to you.'

Why had he had to spoil it? Sally asked herself as she watched his leanly fit body disappear down the stairwell. She had almost begun to like him, the gentle side she hadn't known existed, but now dislike raged again in her. Could he only be human and civilised when she was on the point of bleeding to death? Irritated, she threw back the quilt and swung her feet to the floor, then paused before getting to her feet.

For a man who had come to remote Rock Island to write a book, it couldn't have been a palatable thought to take over the running of a lighthouse with its constant dedication to time intervals. The last thing he had needed was for a female journalist to descend on what little time he could devote to his writing, moreover one who had destroyed an afternoon's work by cutting herself with an axe and made it necessary for him to stay in the main house where his typewriter wasn't. She had no doubt whatsoever that he had kept his promise to stay close by.

She rinsed her face awkwardly with one hand and combed her hair the same way before going downstairs and making her way into the kitchen.

'You'll only need one hand to eat this,' Lyle told her, putting at her place a colourfully assorted plate of coral pink salmon, green peas, and a generous

portion of scalloped potatoes in a rich creamy
sauce.

'You made this?' she asked incredulously—and
inanely, she realised a moment later.

'Producing a reasonable meal isn't difficult when
there's a well stocked freezer and a supply of
packaged goods,' he said drily, taking his place opposite and picking up the glass of white wine he had
already poured. 'Here's to your speedy recovery.'

Sally blinked, strangely unnerved by the cutting
edge of his voice which never seemed far from the
surface in his conversation. Except for those few
minutes of grace when she had needed gentleness
from him. Her mouth firmed as she picked up her
fork and eased off a portion of the succulent fish.
She wasn't enjoying the prospect of spending the
next week stranded with him on this godforsaken
island any more than he relished her company
there.

'Can I get a message to my boss in Seattle?' she
put abruptly, and saw his mouth quirk wryly up at
one side.

'I can send a message for you, but there's no
hurry for that, is there? They're not expecting you
back for several days yet.'

'I'm supposed to attend the Governor's levée on
the twenty-third.' If she had expected him to be
impressed by that piece of information she was
sadly disappointed.

'In an official capacity, I presume?' At her nod,
he went on, 'You might still make it.'

'I have to let Jerry know there's a possibility I
might not,' she insisted stubbornly. 'He'll need time
to arrange for someone else to go in my place.'

'Jerry,' he mused, eyes sardonically thoughtful as he wielded his fork then looked speculatively across at her. 'What is he?—fair, fat, forty and bald?'

'No, he isn't,' Sally snapped defensively, rising to his bait. 'As a matter of fact, he's fair, slim, far from forty, and he has a fine head of hair!'

'Mmm.' The speculation deepened in his eyes. 'From your spirited defence, I'd say he was a lot more than your boss, am I right?'

'No, you're not!'

'Ah, methinks you protested a little too vigorously there,' he came back, amused in a sly way that flicked Sally on the raw.

'We're friends, Dr Hemming, good friends.' Her tone changed vehemence to sweetness. 'But you wouldn't know anything about that kind of relationship between a man and a woman, would you?'

His brows shot up in what she was sure was pretended surprise. 'I have lots of women I count as— friends. Good friends,' he stressed, his eyes lit in their depths by a sarcastic glow of humour.

'Like the blonde I saw you holding hands with at Harvey's Club?' she threw out without thinking, and was gratified to see a jolt of shock that passed over his hard-formed features, even if it lasted for only a second or two.

'Ah, yes, Magda,' he drawled then. 'It has to have been her, because I've never taken another woman there. Yes,' he nodded blandly, 'I'd class Magda as a very good friend.'

'We're not talking on the same wavelength, Professor,' Sally said, crisply short. 'Your classifi-

cation of friend doesn't approximate mine in any
way.' Seeing only too clearly that a continuation
of the conversation on that level could only lead to
a clash of their differing personalities, she changed
tack abruptly. 'Is it possible for me to speak to
Jerry personally?'

'There could be some difficulty in getting
through, better let me see to it.'

His tone had hardened, as if their repartee no
longer amused him, and Sally bit back the objection that rose to her lips. However independent,
however spirited her nature was, intuition told her
not to press Lyle Hemming too far in any one
direction. He was apparently a man of chameleon-
type moods, going from humour to dark cutting
moroseness in one easy motion. But all she had to
do was to bide her time until she was off the island,
well armed with quotes from his literary effort, and
she would hold the whip hand.

They ate their meal in comparative silence after
that, and it was with a sense of relief that Sally
obeyed his instruction to go into the living room
while he washed the dishes she was incapable of
doing with her injured hand and made coffee.

She walked restlessly round the small room,
pausing to stare in mesmerised fascination at the
revolving flash of the light for long moments before
turning back into the room and throwing herself
into her accustomed chair by the fire. All traces of
blood were gone from the hearth, and she felt a
momentary return of compunction when she
visualised Lyle Hemming on his knees cleaning up
the mess made by his unwelcome visitor. She
glanced round the cosy corners of the room.

It was strange that a man of his reputation, locked into the loneliness of this lighthouse station, hadn't taken more advantage of the situation. Yes, he had kissed her—more than that, had made love to her beyond the preliminary stages—but he had been the one to withdraw when she herself would have gone on.

She moved restlessly in the chair, her eyes focusing blindly on the red glow of the fire. Who was she trying to fool by not admitting that she had been like putty in Lyle Hemming's hands, that she would have reached the ultimate with him if the choice had been hers? Only herself.

Her eyes lifted from the fire and went round the room again falling on a well-filled bookcase behind the door. Getting up, she went with a jerky pace and crouched down before the shelves, skimming the titles with frenzied interest. Some were familiar to her from her own modest collection in her apartment, others were of the purely entertainment paperback variety, particularly the mystery novel collection by a writer called John Ainslie.

Extracting one of these, her eyes sharpened with speculation. Could it be?—was it possible that Lyle Hemming used John Ainslie as a pseudonym? He'd certainly have to have one of those, she decided waspishly, if he was turning out this lightest of light fiction for the entertainment of the masses. It sounded like a name he would choose . . . solid, catchy, easily remembered.

She yelped when the door swung back heavily and hit her, and looked up almost guiltily into Lyle's surprised face. His foot hooked the door and closed it, then he moved with the tray of coffee to the low table between the fireside chairs.

'Find anything interesting?'

'There's a lot by John Ainslie,' she said cautiously, getting to her feet, the book still in her hand.

'Lorna's favourite writer,' he said, disconcerting Sally with his indulgent chuckle.

Wouldn't it be natural for his sister-in-law to cherish the books written by her husband's brother? Yet Lyle's attitude was surpremely casual, showing none of the sheepishness she would have expected from a respected professor of English acknowledging authorship. But then, he was nothing like any of the other professors she had known. A man who juggled an involved love life would have no difficulty in keeping a poker face about his literary efforts.

'Has he been writing for long? I've never read any——'

'If you'll excuse me, I have to pay one of my calls on the tower,' he cut in, effectively severing the conversation as he moved to the door and disappeared.

Too effectively?

Sally was thoughtful as she crossed to the table and poured coffee for herself before settling in her chair with the book. It wouldn't have the impact of revealing the true identity of the author of a salacious bestseller, but it would be sufficient to make the University Board look twice at Lyle Hemming's tenure. They were orientated towards scholarly work, not the entertainment of millions.

She was sitting, a strand of her light brown hair wound round her finger, absorbed in the book when Lyle stamped his way back into the sitting room, and she looked up abstractedly when he said,

'More coffee?'

Something in his chilling tone told her that he was letting her know in the most sarcastic way that she ought to have poured coffee for him.

'No—no, thanks,' she refused, watching as his lean fingers grasped the handle of the serviceable pot and spilled the dark liquid into his cup. 'He's not a bad writer,' she indicated the book cradled between the legs she had folded in front of her.

'Oh? Lorna swears by him too, though I'm not familiar with his work.'

There was an edgy note to his voice, but whether it indicated impatience with his sister-in-law's choice or an unwillingness to delve deeper into the subject, Sally didn't know. Realising that the relaxed pose she had assumed was more fitting for the privacy of her own apartment, she untwined her legs and let them rest on the colonial hearthrug while she lifted the book to eye level with her un-injured hand.

'Do you mind?' she waved the book question-ingly, and was perplexed again with his testy answer.

'Not at all. In fact, if you're happy on your own, I'll go and do some work before I turn in.'

She wasn't happy in the least, she realised as soon as he had left the main house, especially as the moaning fog alert started up within seconds of his leaving. But he wasn't the kind of man a girl asked to stay with her because she was nervous in unfamiliar surroundings. He was used to women who faced eerie isolation for love of the men in their lives—his mother, his brother's wife. But Sally was stuck here with no man's love to sustain her, no steely arms to enfold her and make her forget the lonely bleating of the foghorn. A strange kind of disorientation assailed her senses. She was lying in the big bed above, which Lyle occupied alone, and his lips were potently warm against hers, her body yearning towards the hard male comfort of his. Loneliness had no place in that fantasy scene, she was warmed and protected by the man whose body sought hers in the supreme comfort of the senses.

A shower of sparks drew her attention back to the fire, and she got up in a half-dreaming daze to replenish it. How ridiculous it was, she told herself with a wry clarity, to picture Lyle Hemming in a situation like that. He had long ago left the confinement of a lighthouse station and expanded his senses to the wider world beyond. A world where the sensuous part of his nature had taken over, and could he be blamed for that? He was a natural for the adulation of the young women who worshipped at his feet, the older women who saw in his lean good looks a panacea from the men they had known in their lives. Like the blonde, Magda.

She closed the glass doors with more force than necessary and caught up the paperback book before going up to the narrow room that was hers for the duration of her stay. She tried to concentrate on the story that had begun to grip her, comfortable in the cosy warmth that penetrated her room through the open door, but her mind kept straying.

How could he write with the constant interruption of the foghorn shattering his thoughts? Maybe, she decided as she settled under the covers, he was immune to such interruptions. His childhood had been spent in these surroundings, on this island, so of course they meant nothing to him. The words of the book held loosely in her only hand exposed from the bedcovers fused and made no sense, but she was still holding it firmly when she fell asleep.

Daylight was just a pale pink glow on the walls of her bedroom when Sally woke again, and she peered at the luminous dial on her watch. Six-thirty, and there was no sound of movement in the house that perched atop Rock Island.

The foghorn still wailed monotonously, although it ceased suddenly when Sally swung her feet to the bedside rug and glanced across the hall to the open door of the master bedroom. Surely Lyle should be stirring by now, busily recording the latest weather data from the machines he had explained to her the day before?

Owlishly, she got to her feet and padded across the narrow passageway. Blinking, she stared at the smoothly made up bed with its blue counterpane. Lyle wasn't there—hadn't been there if her instincts were correct.

Turning back into her own room, she picked up her jeans and slid into them, then pulled a thick sweatshirt over her head, pulling it down around her hips as she half fell down the narrow stairs and gained the hallway.

The multi-hued green of lichens gave soggily

under her feet as she went quickly across it to the small assistant keeper's cottage to the left of the tower. It wasn't possible that Lyle was neglecting his lighthouse duties, but something drove her on and made her look into the broadest window giving on to the cabin's interior, her hands shielding the dawn light at either side of her face.

The huddled figure on the divan spoke volumes to her agitated mind. He had worked late and overslept his deadline for making the recordings so important to the lighthouse operation.

The door yielded easily to her hand, and she rushed across the small room to where he lay in a sleep that transcended all urgent calls to duty.

'Lyle! Wake up! It's almost seven.'

He stirred, but only enough to throw back the covers from a chest that was naked and reveal a tangled growth of wiry hair reaching down towards his navel. Her eyes went to the piled clothes beside the bed and took in the fact that he was sleeping naked. She gave an irritated exclamation when the brawny arms reached up and encompassed her waist, pulling her down to the yielding springs of the mattress.

'Oh!' she gasped, startled when his supple hands slid purposefully up over her ribs and stroked provocatively against her breasts, bringing them to a tingling awareness that sent shooting sensations down as far as her toes, which curled inside her shoes as if drawn on a puppet string. 'Lyle, you've got to come! Please—you've got to take the recordings!'

The dullness of that proposition did no more than rouse him to a closer clutch on her person, his hands moving with a swiftness that amazed her down to the hem of her top, then pushing up under its thick folds to find the soft peaks of her breasts, groaning his appreciation as his hands moulded them to receptive awareness.

'Oh, forget it!' she snarled as she pulled away and got to her feet. If he wouldn't attend to his responsibilities, then somebody must.

The inner sanctum of the tower, when she came into it, panting, was a maze of machinery that struck horror to her innermost soul. The steady click of data accumulation intimidated her for long, paralysed moments, and then she moved jerkily towards the semi-circle of modern technology. Her hand picked up the indelible pen beside the journal that recorded vital information, and paused before entering the time of recording.

'6.30 a.m.' she wrote, imitating Lyle Hemming's bold black strokes in the entry above. Meticulously, she recorded the readings on all the instruments indicating weather and cloud condition, drawing from the information she had absorbed from Lyle's orientation lecture the day before. Amazed by the extent of the knowledge she had retained, her strokes became bolder until no one but an expert would know that she, and not Lyle Hemming, had made the recordings.

'What the hell do you think you're doing?' the harsh voice broke in on her complacency as she stood back to admire her handiwork.

She swung round to confront Lyle Hemming's indignantly contorted features. 'I'm doing the job you should have seen to an hour ago,' she retorted sharply.

'Who the hell asked you to?' he demanded belligerently, pushing her aside while his yellow-toned eyes went from one machine to the other.

'Nobody,' she conceded bitterly, stepping back out of the range of his outraged fury. 'And I really don't give a damn whether the coastguard believes the entries or not. I did what I thought was best——' To her horror, her voice came out in a plaintive justification of her actions, and she pulled away from the hand he had placed like a vice on her wrist. 'A little gratitude wouldn't be out of order, Professor!'

His eyes went from the instruments to her neatly inscribed figures in the ledger, coming up to meet hers as his hand raked through his thick dark hair, mussing it even more than the effects of sleep had.

'I'm sorry.' To her amazed ears, he even sounded a little contrite. 'I guess I took out my anger at myself on you. I—appreciate what you tried to do.'

Tried? New indignation bubbled inside her and erupted with her gritted, 'Would you like to check my work, Dr Hemming? As you said yourself, it's not a job that requires great intellect, just an application to duty.' She noted that he had the grace to flush under the heavy growth of dark hair on his face when she stressed the last words.

'Don't worry yourself, Miss Brown,' he flicked tersely, moving past her to bend over the instruments, 'you won't have to stretch your intellect to its limits again—on Rock Island, at least.'

'Oh!' she breathed, incensed, and flung away from him towards the stairs, her heels rattling on the steps the only sound that filled her mind. Tears of anger blurred her vision as she fled from the round tower to the mossy rocks beyond it.

'God, how I hate his kind of man!' she sobbed half aloud, only the uncaring screech of resident gulls making note of her alien presence.

CHAPTER FIVE

SHE had made her bed and eaten a sparse breakfast of coffee and toast when Lyle Hemming put in an appearance. He had shaved, she noticed in one encompassing glance, and changed into a heavy flannel workshirt of mid-brown and thick twill pants of the type he had worn the day of her arrival.

'I've sent a message to be relayed to your boss,' he said without preamble, 'also one to your parents.'

'My parents?' Her head swivelled on an acute angle. 'I didn't ask you to do that.'

'No, but there's always a possibility that you won't make it back there for the Christmas holiday. I assumed you'd planned to spend it with them?'

She gave a curt nod and his jaw tightened as he went to the stove area and took a mug from the cupboard above it, pouring coffee and carrying it back to the table without looking at her again.

And maybe that was as well, Sally told herself, biting her lip in frustration and a strange sense of dread. Keeping men in the place she had assigned to them had never been a problem before, but the Professor was something else again. Nothing in her experience had prepared her for living in close proximity to a man like him. For a woman, there were no other choices than either loving or hating him. While her mind was telling her one thing, her body

was betraying her with its too-vivid memories of
his lovemaking, of the warm evocation of his
caressing hands stroking expertly where they had
no right to stroke.

'Look, I've said I'm sorry,' he said now from the
table to her averted back, a tinge of impatience
edging his voice. 'The recordings you did this morning were fine, I couldn't have done better myself.'

'Thank you kindly, sir.' She spun round on her
heel to face him, her hands spreading behind her
to grasp the lipped edge of the counter top. 'It's
comforting to know that my university education
stands for something.'

'Oh, for God's sake,' he said wearily, 'of course
it stands for something. I'm hopeful it's taught you
to think creatively for yourself and that because of
it you can make a valid contribution to the society
you find yourself in.'

'And didn't I do that this morning?' she challen-
ged.

'Yes, you did.'

'Then——?'

'Then—what?'

'Why can't I take over part of the responsibility
for the lighthouse?' she pursued, sudden enthusiasm propelling her feet across the kitchen, coming
to a halt opposite him. Earnestly she went on, 'I'll
go mad stuck on this lump of rock if I don't have
something constructive to do. Why can't I free you
to get on with the book you came here to write?'

He stared up at her thoughtfully, his yellow-
brown eyes giving consideration to her proposition.
Finally he shook his head negatively. 'The responsibility is mine.'

'All right, the final responsibility can be yours,' she said, exasperated. 'You can be there to make direct reports, and I'll take care of some of the other ledger reports. Nobody outside needs to know that you're not personally on duty twenty-four hours a day.'

For a moment she was sure he would veto her suggestion; the frown slicing between his dark brow promised this. But after what seemed an interminable pause, he lifted his eyes levelly to hers.

'All right,' he nodded. 'You can take the first twelve hours, I'll take the dark hours shift. From your performance this morning,' he injected a note of wry humour into his voice, 'I'm assuming that you're an early morning person, which I, regrettably, am not.'

A triumph that was shortlived shot through her. She had madeer point of being capable of performing a viable role in the rugged world of light-housing, but that emancipation also entailed a life spent in solitary command during the daylight hours when Lyle worked or slept. She hadn't expected him to give in so easily to her demand, and that set a whole new hornets' nest of speculation buzzing in her mind. Would he have given in that easily to a blonde Magda, knowing that their hours of togetherness would be strictly limited?

The question flitted in and out of her mind so quickly that she was scarcely aware it had occupied her thoughts. More lasting was her sense of relief that her encounters with the Professor would be minimal from now on. Whatever her sensual awareness insisted on, she knew his kind of man was poison to a woman with her self-imposed standards of the man who would fill her life. She wanted, needed, the kind of fidelity her parents knew, the one-on-one situation where loyalty was never questioned. A facet of life, she reminded herself bleakly, that Lyle Hemming and his kind didn't even pay lip service to.

Sally hadn't realised—hadn't given much thought to—the magnitude of the job she had taken on. As Lyle had told her at the beginning, recording data in the ledger required little in the way of mental acumen. What wore away at her optimism, like water drops on stone, was the desolate isolation of it all, the eerie aloneness she felt each time she entered the tower and made her way up to the central core.

Wind had replaced the still calmness of enveloping fog, and was far more menacing to her ragged nerves as it battered its fury against the solitary tower, shaking it until Sally feared for the stability of its foundations. Frightening enough in the less fortified main house, the wind assumed otherworld dimensions as it shrieked and howled round the upthrust of the light tower. Braving its vindictive snatching at her clothes as she crossed, head down, to make the necessary annotations in the log book, Sally wondered often at the sanity of people who made their living from this life.

But nothing short of green-skinned monsters from another galaxy would have persuaded her to make a complaint to Lyle Hemming. Something— she wasn't entirely sure what—made her keep her fears silent when she ate the one meal of the day she shared with him.

He seemed oblivious to the storm raging around them, and more than once Sally silently cursed the stoicism of his mother and his sister-in-law, immured as they had apparently been to the stormy chaos on Rock Island.

The conviction grew in her that he was testing her in some obscure way, gauging her ability to stand up, as they did, against anything nature could throw at them. Her three-hourly trips to the tower became the focal point of Sally's existence, the life she lived between becoming a marking-time until the clock hands told her it was time for another pilgrimage.

A variety of board games after the evening meal provided a welcome relief, coinciding as they did with the relinquishing of her responsibility towards the lighthouse operation. Lyle himself relaxed over concentration on the backgammon board, his long fingers making maddeningly correct moves that resulted, more often than not, in his emerging triumphant from the game.

Oddly, being consistently beaten made Sally nonetheless eager for their next encounter. The main house became like a jailer during the daylight hours when Lyle secreted himself in the assistant keeper's house and wrote. She craved company, even the disturbing presence of the man who continued to bedevil her senses, making them swing wildly first one way, then the other. The flexibly mobile lips became as deeply imprinted on her memory as the pale familiarity of her own fingers flitting over the board, moving her men into strategic positions. She even felt mild surges of jealousy about the work he devoted so much time to.

On the fourth night of her confinement on the island, a particularly venomous swoop of wind rattled the window panes in the sitting room, and Sally shivered as she glanced back across her shoulder. 'It's like some kind of monster trying to get in,' she whispered.

'Are you afraid of it?' The surprise in his voice whirled her back to face him over the low table.

'Of course not,' she flared sarcastically. 'My nerves are perfectly used to the idea that at any minute the house I'm sitting in could be lifted bodily and sent out to sea!'

A spark lit his eyes, but he said evenly enough, 'The house has stood here for a long time, and in far worse storms than this.' He got to his feet and looked thoughtfully down at her. 'If I seemed surprised that a wind should bother you it's because you've never shown any lack of courage while you've been here. There's no other woman I know who would have taken on what you have; a lighthouse in a storm isn't everybody's cup of tea.'

He turned away with an abruptness that belied the words of admiration, and Sally stared after him as he went out of the room. It was almost as if he was ashamed of admitting to any kind of appreciation for a member of the opposite sex, except in the most basic way possible. Was that it? Had he been so spoiled by the adulation of women that he no longer respected them as valuable, thinking people?

'Here, drink this.' He came back into the room and handed her a glass with brandy to the half level. 'Your nerves will appreciate it even if your prissy soul doesn't.'

Her fingers tightened round the stem of the glass, her knuckles growing white. 'Why do you keep calling me prissy?' she asked quietly.

'Aren't you?' he prevaricated, a faint smile round his mouth as he looked down into his own glass, dark lashes obscuring his eyes.

'I don't believe so, no.'

'Don't misunderstand me. There's more than one way of being prissy. However much a woman— sleeps around—she can still hark back to the pro- verbial old maid in her judgment of others who do the same thing.'

Sally drew in her breath on an indignant hiss, then blindly raised the glass to her lips and took an eye-watering gulp of its fiery contents. When she was able to speak, she gasped, 'You—you're insulting!'

'Why?'

'Why? Because—because I don't sleep around, Professor, as you so delicately put it.' Her ire and the brandy had put a high colour in her cheeks, and her eyes sparkled contemptuously at him as he towered above her. It was like an electric shock when he lifted his head and stared directly into her moss-green eyes.

'No?' he said softly.

'No!'

'Then you're a paragon among your profession, Sally Brown. But I have to admit I find that hard to believe after our—moments of closeness.'

'You really are insufferable!' she gritted through her teeth and, unable to contain herself any more, leapt to her feet and glared at him on a more even footing. 'You bear the worst kind of prejudice, labelling people because of what they do. Maybe there are journalists and reporters who play the field, men as well as women, just as there are in any other trade or profession, but I don't happen to be one of them.' Her feet moved her a step closer to his tautly held figure. 'And I know dozens of others in my profession who have more morality in their big toes than you, Professor, have ever possessed!'

She was beside herself as a rage she had never known before rocketed through her, and she was unprepared for the reach of his arm that snaked round her waist and drew her to him. She was vividly, shockingly aware of the bland warmth of his firm chest against the delicate curve of her breasts, the hard contours of his thighs pressing hers.

'Am I supposed to say you're beautiful when you're angry?' he said with a husky amusement that was gone before she had time to react to it. 'Well, you are, Sally Brown . . . very beautiful with that yellow spark in your green eyes . . . skin as soft and dewy as a spring flower . . . a mouth made for a man's kisses. . . .'

She stiffened, her hands pushing against shoulders that were immovable, but the provocative trail of his fingers over her hair, making it feel like silk, and down in a tracing motion over her cheek and jawbone, left her without breath to make her protest. His hands ran provocatively down her back, shivering awareness to life and bringing her trembling lips up to receive the teasing pressure of his mouth.

Her hands gripped on the rough cotton of his

shirt as his kiss deepened and grew lazily into a sensual demand she was powerless to combat. Her hand lifted, drifting up over the rasping jut of his chin to the hair that lay low on his forehead, brushing through its thickness until her fingers clasped and fused with her other hand behind his neck. With expert ease, he parted her warm mouth and drew her pliant body closer to his, her hips fluid under his caressing hands.

She didn't hear the rage of the wind, nor feel its forceful shudders against the foundations of the isolated house. Lost in the world Lyle Hemming had created, she let sensation ripple warmly over her, engulf her, make her mindless of yesterday and tomorrow. Her head lifted to expose her throat when his mouth finally left hers, and she moaned as his lips traced provocative fire over the tender whiteness of her skin and lodged at the indentation where she felt her own pulse leaping erratically.

Then he was raising his head, lifting away from her, and she clutched at the rough fabric of his shirt, willing him to go on.

His voice was huskily unsteady when he looked down into her eyes and said, 'I have to go over to the tower now. Do you want me to come back?'

Sally knew what he was asking. He had slept in the assistant's cottage for the past two nights, snatching sleep between bouts of working on the book. Now he was asking if she wanted him back here . . . in her bed. Nothing else would be possible . with the intensity of the feelings they had roused in each other. Dazedly, she met his gleaming, tawny eyes and nodded inarticulately.

The whole room, the house, seemed possessed of

a waiting quality when he had left it, reflecting the
inner suspension Sally knew. She had been waiting
for Lyle Hemming all her life, she realised with a
thrill of recognition. He was her knight in shining
armour, the epitome of all her girlhood dreams. A
tarnished knight, perhaps, in some ways, but who
had ever heard of a knight with monkish qualities?
The women he had known before her had meant
nothing to him in any real sense, a marking time
until this night when love would be the supreme
experience it was meant to be.

Love, she mused, her mouth smiling tentatively
as she piled logs into the fireplace and closed the
glass doors on them. The most startling moment
of all had come when she realised that she had
loved Lyle all along, that her antipathy towards
his way of life had been no more than jealousy
spawned by resentment of her own exclusion from
his life. She was, and always had been, as besotted
with him as any of the fawning girls in his
classes.

Dreamily she went up the narrow stairs to her
room. Now, it seemed as if she had been aware of
him for ever, that she had unconsciously compared
current male friends to him and found them wanting. One thing was certain, she told herself, pausing
reflectively in the doorway, no other man in her
existence had the power over her that Lyle
Hemming had. She had never been seriously
tempted to stray from the path she had mapped
out for herself, however persuasive the male argu-
ments had been. Her personal future had been
clearcut for a long time . . . marriage to a man she
loved and respected, children to make the union

complete, and the opportunity to pursue her own career.

Her mouth curved into a tender smile. With a background of family women who played a vital role in their husband's professional life, he would never object to his wife being. . . .

Wife! She moved away from the door and went into the almost claustrophobic confinement of her room, searching for and finding the silky nylon of her nightdress. Lyle had avoided marriage thus far, and there was no indication that he intended to change that status. Sally clutched the nightdress to her, her fingers whitening with tension. For heaven's sake, he hadn't even mentioned that he loved her, or cared for her in any special way. But that wouldn't be his style.

Was she making herself too available? The thought lodged in her brain and stayed there all through her undressing and while she scrubbed her teeth in the bathroom along the hall. By agreeing that Lyle should come back to the main house that night, she had told him that she was willing to spend the night with him. She couldn't have virginal vapours now—a man like him would scar her with his mockery if she fought him off on those grounds.

She emerged from the bathroom just as he sprang lightly up the stairs and turned in the passage to look at her. Her doubts fled as if they had never existed when his eyes went down over the revealing contours of her nightdress, then back up to her face and the cloud of light brown hair surrounding it.

'Oh God, you're beautiful,' he breathed reverentially, but he made no move towards her.

Instead, his arms opened and he left the decision up to her whether or not to move into them.

Sally took one step, her eyes luminously fixed on his, then another, and the arms closed round her, making a haven that was comforting yet exciting. Her hands reached up eagerly behind his head as he bent lithely and picked her up, their lips fusing when the dark line of his head dropped to hers. Then he was carrying her . . . not to her own room, she noted vaguely, but to the double-bedded master opposite.

She felt the risen scallops of the bedcover under her when he lowered her on to it, and it seemed her brain was only receptive to her tactile senses . . . the warm sensuality of his mouth as it provoked a wild response wherever it touched, the caress of hands that knew every area of pleasure on her quivering body, the hard press of his hard thighs when he eased over her. The response that shattered every nerve in her left no room for regrets as her hands sought to give the same pleasure to him. Her groan of frustration as her hands encountered the coarse cloth of his shirt brought an immediate response.

'Don't go away,' he said thickly, and she felt a weak desire to giggle when he took his covering warmth from her and stood beside the bed, his clothes rustling as he put them from him. She couldn't have moved if he had announced that a bomb was set to go off under them. Liquid fire ran in her veins, igniting an overwhelming conflagration at the centre of her being so that the hands that reached for him as he rejoined her acted only as an automatic response to the clean, hard virility of him. Surprise flared up and died at the silky quality of his skin as her hands stroked the hard-muscled flesh of his shoulders and back. Fleetingly, she wished for his eloquence as he murmured against her mouth, her throat, the alert rise of her breasts, but her voice seemed lost in the wild roar that deafened her.

'Lyle, please,' she found her voice at last through the disorientated swim of her senses, 'I—I've never done this before.'

'What?' He lifted his head from the rounded thrust of her breast and stared at her bemusedly. 'What did you say?'

'I've—never slept with a man before,' she said on a half-sigh, then drew in a startled breath when he cursed and rolled to one side.

'This is a fine time to tell me something like that,' he rasped, his head turning alertly when an unreal light flickered whitely round the room.

'What was that?' Sally asked fearfully as the light repeated itself. It couldn't be the light tower, that was more of a yellow glow that flashed intermittently into this bedroom at the front of the main house.

'Somebody's in trouble,' Lyle grunted, leaping from the bed and hurriedly drawing on the clothes he had discarded only minutes before. 'Stay in the house,' he ordered briefly, and then he was gone, rattling down the stairs two at a time, pausing momentarily at the front door before slamming it loudly behind him.

Sally sat up, her pulses beating erratically as another white glare filled the room. What did 'in trouble' mean on a night like this? The folds of her nightdress fell round her as she jumped from the bed and ran across to the small-paned window. Beyond the blinding revolution of the tower light, everything was dark as pitch.

A light bobbed suddenly on the cliff top to her right, and she barely discerned Lyle's shadowy figure behind it. The wind, which had been screaming without her hearing it for the past while, rattled the window panes and she stepped back involuntarily. God help anyone out in a boat on a night like this, she thought devoutly, concerned for the faceless men she imagined tossing on the ocean's lashing whitecaps.

Clasping her arms around her, she looked at the room cosily surrounding her. Guilt smote her when she visualised how happy the men on that distressed boat would be in the safety of the main house.

Disregarding Lyle's instruction to stay where she was, she leapt over the distance between the main bedroom and hers, pulling off her nightdress as she went. There was no way she could sit quietly here while men drowned half a mile from her. Surely there was something she could do?

Lyle's flashlight was already a bobbing pinpoint far below when, dressed warmly in thick pants, sweater and pile-lined jacket, she stood peering down from the cliff top. Blessing the foresight of the permanent keepers in providing a multitude of flashlights easily available in the main house, Sally shone the ray down the cliffside, catching Lyle in its beam before flashing it outwards to the ocean.

There were no more flares being set off to denote the boat's position, and the flashlight beam illumi-

nated only the rocky shore area through a mist of
spume thrown up by the cascading waves. She
swung the light back to Lyle and vaguely saw that
he had gone down from the steps to the rock pin-
nacles below them. He looked dangerously near the
frothing fury of the waves, and without thinking
she started down the steps screaming his name, her
throat rasped to hoarseness before she realised that
the wind was effectively sweeping her words into
oblivion.

Halfway down she missed the edge of the step
and only saved herself from pitching forward when
she grabbed for the handrail, fortunately on her
right, though the action was so automatic that she
would have grasped it with her injured hand. The
flashlight dropped from her hand and rolled across
the step and disappeared without a sound between
the risers. The wind howled and swooped around
her, greedily snatching at her breath as she steadied
herself against the rail and peered down into the
darkness. Was the distressed boat still out there, or
had it been swept past them to the projection of
rocky foreshore to the south? If it had, as seemed
likely, Lyle was risking his life down there for no
reason.

Sally felt her way more cautiously down the
steps, her hair blowing wild strands into her eyes
and mouth. It seemed years before her feet touched
down on the level plankway of the landing station,
and she paused again to draw breath. Lyle was
waving his flashlight back and forth in an arc, and
she marvelled at his faith in there being survivors,
let alone ones who would wash up on this particular strand of shoreline.

'Lyle!' she screamed against the wind, and saw the light waver momentarily as he turned back to look at her jacketed figure clinging to the rail. He shouted something like 'Go back!' but Sally stepped down on to the rocks like a woman with a mission and edged her way towards him.

Water was foaming over her feet when at last she reached the boulder he stood on, and his face expressed a vicious anger as he glanced down at her.

'What the hell are you doing here?' he shouted, his arm still moving rhythmically. 'I told you to stay where you were.'

Balancing on the flat-topped rock, she brushed vainly at the hair whipping round her face. 'Come back with me, Lyle!' she screamed hoarsely. 'There's nothing out there now.'

He said nothing, but directed his grim gaze out along the flash of the light's beam so purposefully that her eyes followed his and saw what he had known all along. A fishing ketch loomed eerily out of the darkness, and was briefly, shockingly, outlined in the spasmodic beam from the tower far above them. Lyle's sharp voice sounded suddenly at her ear.

'Get back and stay out of the way! I've more to think about than your safety!'

She twisted her head to look at him, and saw the relentless coldness in his eyes. Turning without a word, she groped her way back to the stair platform and gripped the rail tightly with her hands as she leaned against it and watched the drama unfolding before her. At that moment she had no thought for the real-life impact such a story would have in her lighthouse article. She was solely, completely, a woman in love who watched her man risk his life for the saving of others. She didn't even feel resentful of his high-handed ordering of her out of the area of danger. Wasn't that what any man in love would do? The fact that Lyle Hemming loved her brought a warm glow inside her that seemed to magically ward off the stark horror of the next minutes.

She stared at the now visible lines of the ketch, seeing the puppet-like figures of the crew as they battled uselessly against the storm. Her heart jumped into her throat and stayed there when the splintering of wood superseded even the wind's fury, and then everything started happening so quickly that she had no time to marshal her wire-taut nerves and think coherently. She heard the frantic yells of one, two, three crew members who groped vainly at the rocks before being swept out of sight by the powerful suction of the ocean. Her hands flew to her ears in a vain effort to shut out those dying cries, but something inside her registered that she never could forget those last screams for help.

A help that Lyle, stretched flat on the rocks tumbling down on the foreshore, was doing his best to provide. His hands reached out into the sucking abyss under him, coming up with two of the crew at one moment, then with the next surge of the ocean pulling only one to the safety of the rocks. Sally was helpless, crazed with her inability to do anything, when a movement to the right of Lyle brought her hands from her ears, her eyes to widened alertness.

Her feet slid on the slimy moss of the rocks as she dived down from the platform and made a precarious way to the head she had seen bobbing up and down between the swirl of converging waters. Falling, she scarcely felt the sharp graze of the razor-edged rocks as she got up on all fours and crawled her way to the spot where she had seen the crewman's head. Stretched at full length, as Lyle had been, she moaned as she stared frantically down into the swirling foam. He had gone, the man she had thought to rescue. There was no trace. . . .

She cried out again in exhausted triumph when the dark outline surfaced again, and she put down both hands to grasp the sodden dark jersey of the man who seemed more dead than alive.

'Lyle!' She seemed to have spoken in no more than a whisper, yet Lyle suddenly made his presence known by lying beside her and lightening the man's weight from arms that felt as if they were being pulled from their sockets by the surging tide.

'Pull when I tell you,' she heard him say, but her hands seemed frozen in the turgid swirl of the water and her limbs were incapable of co-ordinated movement when the order came.

Rejecting the sob of hopelessness that rose inside her, she steadied herself for the repeated instruction she knew would come.

'Pull now!'

Afterwards she would tell herself that there was humour in the landing of a six-foot-plus male on to the safety the island's rocks provided, but when it actually happened she found herself floundering like a beached whale as breath pumped its way

back into her gasping lungs. Everything took on a
surreal aura, and she only vaguely recalled later
the eternal ascent up to the rocky plateau that
housed the tower and dwellings.

Still more unreal was what happened when she
reached the top. She felt herself being lifted and
carried, the calm in the sudden abatement of the
wind, and much later the wet clothes being stripped
from her body. Her hand was taken up and re-
bandaged to the accompaniment of heartfelt male
curses, so that she knew she had failed in something
. . . it must have something to do with the dying
cries that filled her disorientated mind. Couldn't
she have saved them? The angry voice ministering
to her certainly seemed to think so.

'I—I'm sorry,' she whispered placatingly. 'I tried
to. . . .'

More oaths interrupted her apology, but they
were spoken with a lot less vehemence. Hands
lightly caressed her face and drew back her hair
from her brow and then, as she faded into black
unconsciousness, lips touched her forehead and her
mouth . . . lips more tender than any she had ever
known before. . . .

CHAPTER SIX

THE raucous calls of the gulls woke Sally from a sleep that was as deep and profound as any she had known. She lay blinking in the light that fell greyly into the narrow confines of her room, and she recalled vaguely that she was on an assignment for the magazine.

Throwing back the covers, she stepped from the bed and went to the window in the corner of the room. The sight that met her eyes brought clarity swiftly to her clouded brain. Gulls swooped low over the uneven rocky terrain, uttering their plaintive cries as they settled disgruntledly on the stony outcrops that comprised their dwelling place. She was here, on a place called Rock Island, to complete the series on her article about North Pacific Lighthouses. It took only a few more convolutions of her brain to remember that a man called Lyle Hemming was in charge of the lighthouse, and that disaster had struck Rock Island the night before.

Her fingers curled into her palms as she recalled that they had been fixed like cement to the sweater of a wrecked seaman. Pain pulsed through the reopened surface of her wound as a surge of hopelessness spread through her. How many of the crew had been rescued from the storm that had enveloped Rock Island the night before?

Dreading, yet needing to find out, she washed

and dressed awkwardly in jeans and loose shirt of green and white check. She had kept her eyes averted from the main bedroom on her journeys to and from the bathroom ... that conjured up a far different picture, one she was strangely reluctant to face right now. It was only when, dressed, she stepped into the passage that she saw the mounded hump in the master bed, a stillness that struck horror to her soul. Had the occupant defied death at the hands of the ocean only to succumb here in the warm safety of the main house?

Slowly she approached the bed and saw the bright shock of blond hair long before the eyes opened to stare uncomprehendingly at her. They were the bluest eyes she had ever seen, like spring violets after a rain.

'Hi,' she offered awkwardly, 'how do you feel?'

'A lot better for seeing you, I'll tell you!' The dew-drenched eyes warmed appreciatively as they went lazily down to the vee shape of her shirt and lingered on their way back to the concerned green of her eyes. 'I must have drowned and gone to heaven!'

A shudder sent goosebumps across Sally's skin. 'Don't joke about it,' she said sharply. 'If Lyle hadn't rescued you, you'd be——' She choked on telling him that he'd be ten fathoms under, like most of his shipmates.

'Lyle? Is he your husband? Aw, come on now, don't tell me my dream girl's married.'

'I'm not married,' she told him crisply, stepping back from the bed as if he had a contagious disease. 'Lyle Hemming is in charge of the lighthouse while his brother's away—it's John Hemming who actually runs the light station.'

'So this Lyle is a stand-in?' The blue eyes darkened seriously. He sprang up in the bed and grasped her wrist in a bone-grinding crush, making her aware not only of his strength but the fact that he was nude, at least as far as his waist. A riot of blond hair cascaded over his chest and made him seem more potently virile than his circumstances warranted. 'Who else has been fished out of the sea?—Captain Bradshaw, Phil Corning, Jack O'Neil?'

Sally shrank back from the intense appeal in the bright blue of his eyes. 'I—I don't know,' she confessed truthfully. 'I was just on my way downstairs to find out. I—was pretty well done in when—when it was all over.'

The thick, fair brows contracted. 'Am I to take it from that that you took part in the rescue operation?' he asked in mocking incredulity.

'No, not really.' Sally pulled her hand forcibly away.

'Yes, really,' another voice spoke from the doorway, and her head whipped round to meet Lyle's tawny eyes, the deeply etched lines round them and his grimly held mouth sparking an upsurge of protectiveness in her. But her voice seemed jammed in her throat, and she watched numbly as he stepped tiredly to the bed. 'You owe your life to Miss Brown,' he said heavily to the blond giant leaning back against the pillows. 'If she hadn't held on to you until I got there, you'd have been a goner—too,' he ended on a pause, and the other man narrowed his eyes.

'You mean I'm the only one saved?'

'No,' Lyle said heavily. 'Bradshaw made it. The others didn't.'

Sally averted her eyes from the twisted expression of pain on the man's face, then with a muttered expression of sympathy she walked from the room, leaving Lyle to cope with the survivor's distress.

And what distress it must be, she conjectured as she went down to the kitchen and thankfully grasped the handle of the half-full coffee pot. Men who were probably his friends as well as workmates, meeting their fate in one of the worst ways, it didn't bear thinking about. She huddled on a chair, elbows on the table, hands cradling the potent warmth of the coffee. Maybe she should have stayed up there as a moral support for Lyle. He had looked exhausted, and there had been no recognition in his eyes for the intimacy that had been between them.

Was that surprising? Hardly, in view of the events that had taken place since they had lain together in the bed now occupied by a blond stranger. Sally wouldn't be romantically inclined herself if she had spent the entire night taking care of injured parties ... she was sure that was what Lyle had done. No man could look that washed out even after a few hours of snatched sleep. And she had added to his burden by passing out when he needed her most. She started when he spoke from the entrance.

'Care to pour me a coffee?'

Sally jumped up, her eyes quickly scanning his drained features. 'I'd be glad to—here, sit down and I'll bring it to you.'

She pulled out the chair he normally occupied at the table and dashed over to the coffee pot, extracting a china mug from the cupboard above it and filling it with the potent brew.

'Thanks,' he acknowledged wearily, and lifted it instantly to his mouth.

For what seemed the first time in her life, Sally was inexplicably shy when she resumed her seat opposite. The physical and emotional response she had felt for this man last night still filled her memory, but it was a memory overriden by the stark reality of what had come later. Her hands were unsteady as she cradled her cup again.

'How—how did he take it?' she managed, and saw Lyle's shoulder lift in a hopeless shrug.

'How does any man take it when he finds out that only two out of the six aboard survived the wreck? I imagine he's going to feel damn guilty for the next little while, wondering why it was him, not them, who got the gift of life.'

Her eyes widened as they gazed across at his bent head, the dark arc of his lashes contrasting with the paleness of his skin. He sounded as if . . . as if he had penetrated the blond stranger's skin and knew exactly what he was feeling, would feel. But it was more than that. . . .

'Have you eaten?' she said practically.

'No, I——' He looked up, the tawny light faded in his eyes. 'It's more important that Bradshaw and Nielsen get back to ordinary life. I gather Bradshaw was the captain of the fishing boat, and he's completely disorientated by what's happened.'

Sally put down her cup and got to her feet again.

'He probably is,' she said crisply, going to the drawer under the stove and extracting a heavy iron frypan, 'but you still have a job to do here, regardless of what went on last night.' A thought struck her, and she swung round from the open door of the refrigerator. 'Did you take the readings early this morning?'

'Yes,' Lyle assured her, seeming amused. 'It *is* my responsibility, you know.'

'A healthy dose of responsibility is good for a person,' she rejoined smartly, extracting packaged bacon and eggs from the refrigerator's interior, 'but too much can be a case of overkill. How do you like your eggs?'

There was a definite hint of laughter in his, 'Sunny side. Two.' His chair scraped back and he came to stand beside her at the stove, his hand reaching for the coffee pot and, as if the action reminded him, he asked, 'How's your hand this morning?'

Sally laid thick bacon slices in the pan before glancing up at him, a surprised look on her face. 'I haven't really had a chance to think about it yet.' She looked down at the new, tight bandage. 'Bruised and a little numb, I guess, but I'll live. I'm—sorry I was such an idiot last night, I don't know why I passed out, and just when you had more than enough to take care of as it was,' she ended with a wry apology.

'You passed out,' he said, deliberately calm, 'because you tore the wound open again and lost a lot of blood. I just hope our upstairs visitor appreciates what you went through for him.'

'I'm just glad he's alive,' she said simply, and

found it an effort to turn her attention back to the
bacon sizzling in the pan. Her fingers trembled as
they broke the eggs and dropped them in, amazed
that they remained unbroken in perfect yellow
circles. Why didn't he go and sit down again? It
was hard enough to cope with an injured hand
without his potent presence immediately behind
her. She drew in her breath when his warm fingers
brushed aside the thick fall of her hair and she felt
his lips, softly teasing, at her nape.

'Lyle,' she shivered, 'please——'

His response was to turn her into his arms and
bury his face against her neck, holding her so close
she could scarcely breathe. 'Lyle,' she whispered
his name again, but it was a faint offering that
faded into nothing when his lips began a feverish
trail across her skin, then covered hers with an
intensity that brought an immediate—and devastating—response. Her arms wound round his
shoulders, and she surrendered to the deep wave of
wanting that flooded from him to her, even glory-
ing in the searing rasp of his unshaven chin against
the tenderness of her own. It was wild, unexpected,
and somehow immoral with a shipwreck just hours
behind them, but she loved it, loved him with every
tingling fibre of her being.

'Are you planning to finish us off by letting the
house burn down?' a harsh voice splintered between them, and Sally's head whipped round first
to the doorway and then, with a gasp, she turned
to the pan still sizzling on the stove. Acrid blue
smoke rose from the charred remains of Lyle's
breakfast, and she automatically put out her hand
towards it.

'I'll do it,' Lyle said tersely, swinging her clear and, lifting the pan from the stove and turning off the gas simultaneously, he carried the billowing frypan out past the blond stranger to the front door.

Sally's eyes were enlarged with shock when they rested on the figure which at some other time might appear comical. The giant-sized chest was still bare, but his lower half was covered by a draping sheet. The flinty quality in the bright blue eyes, however, would have effectively doused even a hint of hysterical laughter. Those eyes that went over her now, missing nothing of the wild flush in her cheeks, the trembling cross of her arms around her waist. She was relieved when Lyle came back into the kitchen, albeit without the offending frypan.

'How am I going to cook breakfast now?' she addressed him with unusual helplessness.

'There's another pan here.' Lyle had ignored the blond giant on his return, but now he looked up at him over his shoulders as he took a slightly larger frypan from the oven drawer. 'You should get back to bed; I'll bring you something to eat soon.'

'The hell with bed!' Blue eyes—Nielsen, hadn't Lyle identified him?—strode over to the table in his unconventional garb and sat down heavily in Sally's chair. 'Beds are for dying in, and I sure as hell ain't ready to cash my chips yet. You and your lady-love can get back to business as soon as I've eaten and got my clothes back.'

Lyle's jaw clenched and he took a step towards the glaring stranger, but Sally stepped between them deftly and said, 'Wouldn't you like a coffee while I cook you some breakfast?'

Nielsen's eyes faded from belligerence to a knowing leer. 'Do I get the same service he got while you were cooking his breakfast?' his thumb jerked towards Lyle.

'No, you damn well don't!'

The hard steel in Lyle's voice brought Sally's eyes round on him too, and she doubted if there was any effective action she could take to prevent the brewing showdown between the two men. And a confrontation between them could only end in disaster for Lyle. In the ordinary run of events he was a strong male specimen, but set against the burly fisherman he would come out of it as the intellectual aesthete he was.

'You see, Mr—Nielsen,' she said in desperate last measure, 'Professor—*Lyle* and I are going to be married.'

Avoiding Lyle's eyes after dropping the bombshell, she smiled with sweet demureness at the stranger and saw with heartfelt relief that his expression had changed to one of ashamed embarrassment.

'Well, why the hell didn't you say so in the first place? Look, man, I'm sorry,' he addressed Lyle, standing and holding on to his slipping sheet with one hand while he held the other burly arm out to Lyle. 'I thought you had a nice cosy set-up here with—well, you know.'

The fingers of Sally's right hand curled into her palm, waiting for Lyle's denial, but instead he gripped the other man's hand and said smoothly,

'An understandable mistake under the circumstances. As a matter of fact,' his yellow-brown eyes transferred to Sally's shrinking green, 'we'd just made up our minds to get married when you— arrived.'

The blond giant chuckled in a man-to-man way that grated on Sally's taut nerves. 'So we were what you'd call unwelcome visitors, huh? Look,' he said soberly, his eyes going between Lyle and Sally, 'don't think I don't appreciate all you did last night. I guess I just blew my top a while ago with you two, but it didn't mean anything. It's a hell of a thing for a man to lose his shipmates like that, and. . . .'

'It's okay, we understand. Here, take some coffee with you,' Lyle turned to the pot on the stove, 'and I'll bring your clothes to you after you've eaten breakfast.'

There was a fraught pause when Nielsen finally left the kitchen, one hand clutching the coffee mug, the other holding precariously to the draped sheet that had slid round his hips. Bracing herself, Sally turned to face Lyle, expecting a furious condemnation in his eyes and blinking when she discovered a warm clear glow that turned her knees to water.

'I—I'm sorry, Lyle,' she stammered, coherent thought impossible when he came and slid his arms round her, pressing her to the lean outline of his body that spoke a thousand messages she was too confused to interpret.

'Sorry? Why should you feel sorry? Aren't women usually ecstatic when they get engaged to the man of their choice?'

'Don't joke, Lyle.' She shifted uncomfortably against the body that held every dream she had ever cherished. Love wasn't a mathematical formula ... because one loved one didn't necessarily make a total of two. 'I—just told him that because I—I didn't want a fight developing here.'

'Oh,' he said thoughtfully, his fingers casually stroking down the curving thrust of her breast, arousing her to the point of frustrated madness as she fought against the effects his experienced touch provoked. 'Was what you told me last night true?' he changed tack, his mouth pressing secret kisses on the vulnerable pulse throbbing at her throat.

'Wh-what?'

'That you've never been with a man before,' he murmured against her neck.

'Yes, it—it's true.'

'And you won't settle for anything but marriage, till death do us part, the whole bit?'

'Y-yes.'

'Then maybe we'd better think about that, hmm?' His lips bit softly at her jaw, moving to the sensitive area round her mouth, provoking sensual softness wherever they touched, reducing her mind to a dull ache of longing.

'You—you want to get married?' she asked dazedly. 'To me?'

'If that's the only way I can get you,' he said, lifting his head and giving her a teasing smile, 'and it is, isn't it?' His eyes monitored the varied expressions flitting over her face, and his hand tilted her chin towards him. 'Isn't it?' he insisted huskily, and she felt her head nod in acquiescence. It was, but——

'Somehow,' she said breathily, her eyes glowing like green velvet, 'that doesn't seem so important any more. I—I just want to be with you, Lyle.'

He smiled, the even white of his teeth drawing her attention to his well-shaped mouth. 'I'm not saying I won't want to trespass on those marital rights before the papers are signed, sealed and delivered, but sooner or later you'll be putting the noose round my neck.'

'Noose? What do you mean, noose?' she wrinkled her small nose at him. 'Isn't it just as much a noose for me too?'

'You'd better believe it,' he said thickly, his mouth coming down to cover hers and kiss her with all the expertise she had always associated him with..

But she didn't care about that, she thought feverishly as she pressed eagerly to the hard warmth of his lean body, feeling the rightness of loving him when her soft curves fitted in perfect conformation. He had known many women in the biblical sense, but he had asked her, Sally Brown, to marry him. She moaned her disappointment when at last he pushed her away, keeping his hands on her hips as he said wryly,

'We'll be getting another visit from above if you don't make breakfast for the captain and his Viking.'

Sally giggled; it was an excellent description of the blond giant with his Norse blue eyes. 'All right,' she sighed with undisguised reluctance, 'I'll get it for them. I just hope Nielsen doesn't throw it back in my face if it doesn't meet with his approval.'

'I doubt if he'd do that, he seemed to appreciate your——' the tawny eyes twinkled '——qualities.'

She made a face at him and detached herself from his arms, going to the stove and looking with pretended fright at the waiting frypan. 'I hope I can do it without creating a smokehouse this time,' she said lightly.

'You won't have any distractions this time,' he responded in the same vein. 'I'm beat, so I won't get in your way.'

Sally looked worriedly at him. 'But you haven't had your breakfast yet.'

'My appetite seems to have disappeared suddenly,' Lyle grinned tiredly from the door. 'But I warn you, I'll be hungry as a bear after a few hours' sleep.' He sobered. 'Can you take care of the readings as well as the visitors?'

'Sure,' she smiled, 'don't worry about it.'

It was only when he had gone that she really thought about the fishing boat's captain, whom she hadn't yet seen. What kind of injuries had he sustained? Still, Lyle wouldn't have referred to him as a visitor if he needed medical care of any kind.

Happiness welled its warm glow all over her as she set bacon and eggs to frying and refilled the coffee pot. The last twelve hours had a quality of unreality, of a fairy tale that wasn't really expected to come true. Yet her own particular fantasy had come incredibly within her reach. Lyle Hemming, the respected man of letters, loved her, wanted to marry her. None of her contemporaries at college would believe it, if only for the reason that Sally had always made scathing remarks about the English Department's Don Juan who picked women up and dropped them with the speed of greased lightning.

She herself had seen him at the club with a blonde whose obvious attractiveness even now made her fingers curl hard into her palm. But what did she expect? she asked herself savagely as she crammed bread into the toaster and searched in the cupboards for serving trays. Lyle was a bachelor, and no monk. Women were as much a part of his life as breathing.

But she would be his wife. . . .

She came out of her reverie with a start and saw that the bacon was cooked to crisp doneness, the yellow-centred eggs set to perfection. Transferring them quickly to the plate, she arranged the buttered toast on another and set both plates on the cloth-covered tray. Placing a freshly poured coffee on the tray, she surveyed it in a rapid check. It would have looked better with a floral addition, but Blue Eyes would have to do without that kind of embellishment. He wouldn't, she reflected as she carried the tray upstairs, have appreciated that small gesture anyway. He was as macho as any man she had ever known, more so than most. A man with a lust for life in all its forms.

Feeling like Cinderella pursued by the fateful witching hour, Sally fled across to the tower after providing breakfast for the two survivors of the shipwreck and cleaning up the resulting debris in the kitchen. She had also stolen time to eat a hasty breakfast herself of toast and coffee.

Her eyes went automatically to the faint plume of smoke rising from the assistant's cottage. Lyle had eaten nothing, but sleep had been paramount in his mind when he left the main house.

Something about the still atmosphere on the island lent confidence to her steps across the moss-

covered rocks. She, and she alone, was responsible
for the efficient functioning of the lighthouse—although, she reminded herself as she pulled open
the door into the tower, if there was an emergency
of any kind she would be hopelessly inadequate to
take care of it. As last night.

Her mind dwelt on the captain of the fishing boat
as she wound her way up to the second level. He
had been older than she expected, his grey-streaked
hair matted against the white pillows when she had
carried the tray to him. Something in the deep
laugh wrinkles surrounding his hazel eyes had
reminded her of her father. Although Captain
Bradshaw hadn't been smiling. He had seemed
abstracted when he looked up at Sally's cheerful
entry.

'I've brought you some breakfast, Captain,' she
announced lightly from the door. 'I hope you like
bacon and eggs, because that's what you've got.
And toast. And coffee.'

He waved her away as she approached with the
tray. 'I'm not hungry,' he refused brusquely, and
Sally paused beside the bed. Was it surprising that
a man who had lost the bigger part of his crew the
night before should also have lost his appetite? But
however much he starved himself, it wouldn't bring
back the men who had perished.

'A little coffee never hurt anyone,' she insisted
quietly, placing the tray on the small side table and
sitting on the bed beside his rigidly held body while
she proffered the black coffee. 'Here, drink this,
you'll feel better.'

His hand lifted in a violent motion, but she drew
back the coffee just in time. 'I told you I don't

want anything! Just go away and leave me alone.'

She hadn't gone away, but instead had sat with the coffee cup in her hand, her eyes warmly compassionate as she countered with, 'Your crew members can't appreciate a warm cup of coffee any more, can they? They can't enjoy a breakfast of bacon and eggs and toast. But they don't need those things any more . . . you do. And their wives and children do, too. They're going to need you, Captain Bradshaw, to make sure they don't have to do without the necessaries of life. Wouldn't your crewmen have wanted you to help take care of them?'

He seemed to choke. 'I—can't replace husbands, fathers.'

'No,' Sally countered calmly, 'no one can do that. But you can make sure that they know someone cares about them, that they haven't been left all alone in the world. And I'm not talking about money,' she added gently, 'just a person who cares about them.'

'Oh, God, I care,' he cried out, anguished. 'But they're going to blame me for what happened.'

'How can they blame you for an act of nature? *You* didn't make the wind blow, *you* didn't wreck your boat on the rocks. You had as little to say about it as the men who were lost.'

His shaggy head turned to hers and tears flooded his eyes. 'I'd rather have gone myself than lose those men with families. I—I have no one—my wife died two years ago, I don't care if I live or die.'

'Then shame on you, Captain!' Sally rounded on him. 'You have a very good reason for living, and—and eating this breakfast I've prepared for you.' She waved a hand over the cooling tray. 'You've just inherited a bunch of grandchildren. Are you going to let them down?'

Now, she meticulously recorded the readings from the instruments and realised that the tears she had stemmed then were now flowing freely down her cheeks. Women had been widowed, orphans created, from last night's storm. Yet it didn't have to be a complete loss. Captain Bradshaw would see to that.

The roast she had extracted from the freezer that morning was cooking happily in the oven that afternoon when Lyle made an appearance again, his eyes swollen from the depths of the sleep that had kept him immobile for the bigger part of the day. Sally had been quite prepared to take over his after-dark shift at the tower, but felt a fleeting relief that one chore had been lifted from her shoulders.

An added relief was Nielsen's insistence on accompanying Lyle to the tower for the evening recordings; alert and vital, he had made his voluble presence known in the main house from the moment Sally had returned his dried clothing to him. Like a caged lion, he had paced the narrow confines of the main house before going outside and striding across the rocky island from point to point and side to side. The foundered ship's captain, on the other hand, had stayed in the house and seemed reluctant to have Sally out of sight or sound. It was as if, she reflected with a pang, he was clinging to her as he had to the rocks last night.

His injuries were greater than Nielsen's, mental as well as physical. Like the younger man, he had been stripped of his wet clothing when Sally first saw him, revealing the livid darkness of bruises on his torso, the red of angry scratches from the rocks that had been his salvation. Nielsen, she mused wryly as she went about preparing the meal, would come up like new from any catastrophe that occurred in his life.

'That sure smells good,' he enthused when he returned to the house behind Lyle. 'Seems like you've found yourself a real gem, man. A woman who can cook and looks like a picture in a magazine.'

'Yes, she's a real gem.'

Sally's eyes sought his, but he seemed to avoid eye contact as he voiced his agreement, going over to the fridge and extracting two bottles of beer. 'Want one?'

'Sure.' The blond giant accepted the untopped bottle and raised it to his mouth without benefit of glass. After a fractional hesitation, Lyle did the same thing.

'Why don't you join Captain Bradshaw in the living room?' Sally asked tartly, somehow resenting Lyle's ability to make himself one with a man who was as culturally apart from him as night and day. 'There really isn't room in here for a party.'

Lyle did look at her then, his yellow-brown eyes puzzled for a moment, then he slapped Nielsen's broad back and said, 'You heard the boss, let's get out of her hair.'

The blond fisherman grinned in immediate understanding and led the way out of the kitchen.

He really wasn't the most intelligent man in the world, Sally told herself contemptuously as she turned back to the stove, and that made Lyle's rejection of his own intellect a cultural sin. Her mouth was still pressed into a firm line when Lyle came back into the kitchen.

'What are you trying to do?' he demanded abruptly, subduing his voice in deference to the men in the next room. Gone was the warm glow from his eyes, replaced by a bewildered anger.

'More to the point, what are you trying to do?' Sally threw back crisply. 'Nothing about you suggests a man who has the common touch, so what are you trying to prove by acting like that moron in there?' her head jerked in the direction of the living room.

'What would you suggest I do?' he asked, deadly quiet. 'Give them a lecture on Shakespearean literature?'

'I'd prefer it to what you're doing.'

Silence stretched out between them, a pause filled with unspoken recrimination, until Lyle said tautly, 'You know something? You're a snob . . . the worst kind of snob there is. An intellectual snob who looks down on people less educated than she is. But maybe that's a quality required in journalists and critics. All you look for, all you see, is the surface patina over what's alive below it.'

'I don't!' she flared, the spoon she had been basting the roast with dripping oil as she turned furiously to face him. 'I just don't believe that a man of your quality should bring yourself down to the level of—of that man in there.'

'Thanks,' he said drily, going to the refrigerator

and extracting two more bottles of beer. 'You'll let us know when the meal's ready?'

He went without waiting for her reply, and she slammed the roast back into the oven, biting her lip as she straightened from it. What had got into her? Snobbery of any kind, she had thought, was anathema to her. Yet she had acted on an instinct that welled up from some deep recess within her. Her eyes widened in recognition as she sank into a chair beside the table and gazed unseeingly in front of her.

It wasn't Nielsen she had scorned, for all his rough and ready mannerisms. It was what Lyle was doing, the writing she knew was far beneath his talents, that stuck like a burr in her throat. Oh, she had fastened on the more visible form of Nielsen and his crude ways, but her irritation sprang from a much deeper source. Lyle Hemming had sold his talent to commercialism, to the easy reading of the masses. *That* was what bothered her, not Nielsen. She wanted to feel pride in what he was doing— yes, she admitted it, to receive the veneration of her fellows as they admired Lyle Hemming's scholarly works. Nielsen's crude vulgarity had brought home to her that Lyle's recent work was far from scholarly . . . and it was that she hated.

Dinner would have been a dull affair, she realised reluctantly, without the blanketing aura of Nielsen's conversation. Tim Nielsen, she found out, as his seafaring yarns precluded any other social intercourse, had lived a life of high adventure. The snow-clad slopes of the Inner Passage to Alaska gave way without noticeable change of pace to the palm-fringed shores of southern Mexico.

'We put into Manzanillo with building supplies for the new resort they were building there,' he enthused, 'and I'm damned if they didn't make us free of the port. Man,' he addressed Lyle, 'those women were something else. Ready, able and willing—and boy, were they willing!'

Before Lyle had time to do anything other than chuckle appreciatively, Sally rose to her feet and said frigidly, 'Anyone for dessert? I've made strawberry cream pie.' What did it matter that the strawberries were of the frozen variety, the cream synthetically produced? 'Captain?' she addressed the grizzle-haired seaman who had kept quietly aloof from the conversation.

'No, I——'

'Captain!' she warned imperiously, rewarded when he gave her a reluctant smile.

'Just a little, then,' he agreed.

Sally knifed into the dessert she had laboured over for the bigger part of the afternoon and sectioned off the succulent-looking pie into serving portions. Resentment flared again when first Tim Nielsen, and then Lyle, accepted their portions and attacked them hungrily without a word of acknowledgement. Captain Bradshaw's murmured thanks were a poor substitute, and her eyes flared as they went over the two younger men's bent heads.

Her mind still simmered, albeit on a back burner, as the men devoured the dessert and carried the coffee she had had the foresight to brew into the living room at the front of the house, leaving her with the sickening aftermath of the meal. Although, she reflected wryly as she carried the used dishes to the sink and ran hot water over them, it was a compliment of a sort. Every plate, including the Captain's, was clean as a whistle, evidence of a meal that had been enjoyed to capacity.

Lyle came into the kitchen as she lifted the last of the dishes on to the drying rack. 'I'm going over to the tower for a few minutes, but when I get back I'm going to play a few games of gin with Tim. Think you can keep the Captain occupied with backgammon?'

'Does he play?' she asked coolly, making a production of drying her hands on the towel draped to one side of the stove.

'He plays,' Lyle said tersely, and went towards the door, pausing there to look back at her mutinous expression. 'Look, I'm not all that thrilled myself at having the responsibility of two more people on Rock Island, but they're here and there's nothing I can do about it. There's nothing you can do either, except to have a little compassion for what they're going through. Those men that were lost last night were their friends, their shipmates. They need understanding, not the hellish condemnation you've been giving off!'

Sally stared after him, acrid tears biting at the back of her eyes. So much for the concern she had extended, especially to Captain Bradshaw, all day! Because of her caring, he had come out of the depression that had swamped him this morning, and the fact that he had been able to eat the dinner she had prepared had been a small triumph to her.

Instead of joining the two men in the sitting room, she sat tiredly at the kitchen table, her fingers twined round the handle of the coffe cup she had replenished. Too much had happened too quickly for her system to absorb it. The tragedy at sea had come so soon after the earthshaking discovery that she loved Lyle Hemming, always had. She was edgy, irritable, because she couldn't cope with so much all at one time. What did it matter if Lyle found a contrast to his scholarly work in writing for the mass market? If he *was* John Ainslie of detective fiction fame, was there any shame in that? She herself had become involved in the intricate plot of the paperback she had picked up.

But she knew that, deep down, it was vitally important to know . . . for her.

CHAPTER SEVEN

SALLY did play backgammon with the Captain that night, pleased more than anything else when he won game after game. The restoration of his self-respect, even in that small area, was more important than victory for herself.

The sudden transition from a household of two to one of four, three of them males, made the evenings she had spent cosily with Lyle seem an unbelievable memory. True, their eyes met from time to time across the room, but the intimacy was gone. More than that, Lyle still seemed to be condemning her for the snobbery she had never really felt. In fact she realised that, whatever Tim Nielsen's faults, he possessed a zestful charm that not even the horrors of the last twenty-four hours could dampen. Nevertheless, her voice sounded stilted—'prissy' as Lyle would have called it—whenever she spoke to the blond seaman. She was too conscious of Lyle's interpretation of her every word, she told herself, concentrating again on the game in progress with the Captain.

They had all drunk coffee again and it was almost eleven when Lyle rose and stretched in front of the fire. 'Well, time I went across to tend to my duties,' he said without looking at Sally, 'and then I'm going to turn in.'

'Hey, you haven't had a chance to get together with your fiancée all day,' Tim Nielsen protested, and Sally felt the Captain's surprised eyes rest on her.

'You're engaged to each other?' he queried, obviously puzzled.

'Sure they are,' Tim said heartily, getting to his feet and dwarfing Lyle by his side. 'And we're keeping them from the goodnight kisses they're entitled to, so let's hit the sack, Captain.'

'There's no need,' Lyle stated evenly, walking to the door. 'I'm too beat even for that tonight.'

There was a pregnant pause as they listened to the rustle of his donning of outdoor clothes, but as soon as the outer door closed firmly behind him Bradshaw said apologetically to Sally,

'I'm really sorry about this—I didn't know. It seems we're creating a lot of unnecessary hassle.'

'It doesn't matter.' Sally got to her feet, hiding the sharp dip in her emotional level at Lyle's precipitate departure. 'He's not just the temporary lighthouse keeper, he's a writer as well. I imagine he'll spend most of the night writing when he's not taking weather recordings.'

Tim whistled softly. 'A writer?' he mused, awed. 'Isn't that something? But I guess it's something to do with his work as a professor. He's a real clever guy,' he directed to the Captain, 'but you'd never know it, he's so regular. Who'd have thought it?' he ended, shaking his head in disbelief.

Sally pressed her lips together into a tight line, and looked round when Captain Bradshaw asked quietly, 'You don't seem to approve of his writing—*is* it to do with his work at the university?'

The question posed another in Sally's mind. If she admitted that she didn't know what kind of writing Lyle was engaged on, they would hardly credit that she had agreed to marry him, not knowing that vital area in his life. On the other hand, she *didn't* know what kind of literature he was engaged on . . . she just had a good idea of its nature. That was the way she chose to go. After all, if she should happen to be wrong, what harm could two seamen do with their unverified knowledge?

'Far from it,' she answered the Captain's question, crossing to the bookcase where half a shelf was taken up with the output of John Ainslie. Running a thoughtful finger along it, she added, 'Of course, he can't acknowledge these titles under his own name, the university wouldn't approve of that.'

Tim came up behind her and bent his tree-like body to stare at the books she indicated, breathing an oath as he straightened up and stared at her incredulously. 'You mean *he's* John Ainslie? Hell, I've ready every one of his books, and they're great!' He shook his head again in disbelief, and Sally felt a flicker of alarm.

'Please don't mention the books to him,' she fluttered nervously, feeling she had got in over her head, 'because . . . well, he could lose his tenure at the university if it became known that he . . .'

Tim's interruption was a veritable roar. 'Hell, are you saying that they'd cut him off because he's writing books that ordinary people can understand, that people enjoy?'

Bells rang a clanging warning in Sally's head. She wouldn't put it past the belligerent seaman to launch a one-man crusade against the university authorities who, in his opinion, were denigrating the work of a man he personally admired.

'No, no of course not,' she said wildly, 'it's just that ... well, you must have noticed that he's a very—a very *private* man. He wouldn't want everybody to know who he is because his university work is much more important to him. Please, don't tell him that you know his identity. He'd—blame me for telling you.'

Wouldn't he just! Her mind shrank from the inevitable result of Lyle's knowing that she had betrayed his secret writing life. He would feel, justifiably so, that she had· abused her privilege of trust—not the trust extended to a member of the press, but a personal belief in her integrity. He had asked her to marry him, the ultimate trust a man placed in a woman.

Long after she went to bed she tossed restlessly on its deep-sprung mattress. Why had she been so foolish as to confide her suspicions as fact to the two shipwrecked seamen? Because, the grim answer came, she hadn't been sure enough of his love to trust in its basic simplicity. But was anything in life simple to a man like Lyle? A man who could take his choice among the women who cast themselves at his feet, his for the taking?

Wide-eyed, she stared at the night-dark ceiling, knowing she had finally come to grips with the crux of her problem. What did she have that a dozen or more other women in his life didn't possess? In the stark reality of the night surrounding her, Sally assessed coolly her own assets. Looks average, or a little above, intelligence—average again, considering the world in which Lyle Hemming had his

being. Love, in the sense that he inspired the reality
of every woman's dream? An untold number of
women, she dismissed dolefully, had wanted to be
as close to him as she now was.

The sound of Tim Nielsen's husky breathing sent
her on to her side, blankets and quilt shutting out
the alien presence as she burrowed under them. A
hollow ache deep inside her told her, as she slipped
into oblivion, that none of her self-posed argu-
ments held an atom of defence against the basic
truth. She loved Lyle Hemming, and nothing in
the world would ever alter that.

Sally's own resentment at the confinement offered
by Rock Island was echoed more than once by the
enforced guests in the days that followed. Morning
might bring promise, in the lightening of the east-
ern sky, for an end to their incarceration, but it
seemed inevitable that cloud would follow the first
flush of dawn, the restless movement of the sea
grow to a forbidding surge before the day was no
more than launched.

'When are we going to get out of here?' a restless
Tim Nielsen confronted Lyle when a third sunrise
had briefly lit the rocky contours of the island.

'It shouldn't be too long now,' he replied with a
steady calm that betrayed a childhood dominated
by the vagaries of the weather. 'As soon as it's
possible to land a boat, they'll be here and you'll
be back in circulation.'

His eyes seemed to speak more to Sally than to
the reluctant guests on Rock Island, making her
think that perhaps he would be relieved not only
to shuck the two wrecked survivors but her own

presence on the barren rocks. How she wished that she could dismiss his significance in her life as casually as he seemed to have shucked off her presence! It was as if the coming of the two men had pushed all other considerations from his mind. He was polite—maddeningly so—but there was none of the cosy intimacy they had known in the first few days. She didn't even know, she reflected wryly as she crossed the now familiar path to the tower, whether they were definitely engaged to be married. Lyle had said nothing about that in the intervening days—which wasn't surprising, she conceded, considering that they had never spent a moment alone since the arrival of the shipwrecked strangers.

A strange kind of philosophy enveloped her as she went about her duties of making the necessary weather recordings and providing tastily cooked meals for the three men of Rock Island. Time seemed suspended in a vacuum of non-feeling. She did what was expected of her and floated aimlessly the rest of the time. The only question that broke the surface of her vegetative state was the nature of Lyle's work in the assistant's cottage which took up so much of his time. It became an obsession with her, her mind conjuring up the convolutions of an intricate plot of detection which would certainly involve every moment of his creative time. It came as a shock to her when Lyle announced one day, his eyes reflecting the sheen of achievement, that the book was finished.

She was in the kitchen, peeling potatoes for that night's dinner, when he told her. Her hands stilled on the peeler, she looked round at him and something deep inside responded to the ecstatic light in his eyes, while a dread she was unable to shake off surged below the surface.

'That's great,' she responded with a lack of enthusiasm that immediately communicated itself to him. Oh God, she wanted so much to share in the triumph he thought so obviously was his, but the nagging doubt that assailed her was all too evident in the clouded sheen of her eyes, the taut lines of her body as she concentrated her attention on the potato in her hands.

'Have you any idea,' he asked with deadly quietness from her side, 'what it means to an author to finish a book? To have all the doubts and uncertainties behind him? No,' he turned away disgustedly, 'I guess you don't. Dr Jeffries really did his work on you, didn't he?'

The peeler dropped with a clatter into the sink when Sally turned savagely on him. 'If you mean that Dr Jeffries instilled an appreciation for quality literature in his students, then yes, I guess you're right. Is there anything wrong with expecting quality literature from a man who's supposedly dedicated his life to the art?'

'What makes you think I've sold out quantity for quality?' he whipped back, his mouth a hard line as he glared at her.

'Haven't you done that?' she goaded, unable to help herself. 'Writing a book for consumption by the masses is one thing; writing words that will last through the ages is something else again!'

Her fingers grasped the potato in her hands as if she could wring significance from its brown, indented skin, and Lyle stared his contempt in a reality that was far removed from the peaceful surroundings of the kitchen containing them.

'You're like all the rest of your kind, aren't you?' he whipped back coldly, and she wondered why she had ever imagined that his eyes glowed with an inner light. 'You set yourselves up as arbiters of what's fit for human consumption, and leave no margins for individual taste.'

'I'm not a book critic,' she flared, hard eyes meeting harder.

'No? You could have fooled me!'

With that cryptic remark, he swung on his heel and marched out of the kitchen, even the set of his shoulders conveying the contempt he felt for what he regarded as her lack of tolerance. Anger simmered close under Sally's surface as she reflected that he, not she, should have cleaved closely to standards of excellence in literature, given his university appointment in the Department of English Studies.

She got through the meal, hardly hearing the conversation Tim carried on almost a single-handedly. The obsession that had bothered her for days was now crystallised into a definite plan of action. By some manner of means she was determined to take a look at the finished manuscript, flick through it to extract some of the choicer examples of inferior prose, and make her point in an article she was even now forming in her mind.

Her plans were laid even as they played four-handed card games when the dishes had been cleared from the kitchen table, though despite her distraction she still felt Lyle's eyes rest on her from time to time, his mouth a tight line of disapproval, his eyes bleakly forbidding. She needed no words to know that the marriage was off—had it ever really been on? It had been convenient to make that kind of excuse for Tim's benefit when he surprised them in the kitchen that first morning, but it had been no more than that—had it? The wistful thought crept into her mind and died a sudden death when her eyes met Lyle's. It was as if he hated her.

The problem was, she reflected, selecting a card blindly and playing it, only to get a baleful look across the table from Tim, whose partner she was, that it was almost impossible for her to get into the assistant's cottage at a time when Lyle wasn't there. An island, she told herself wryly, wasn't the ideal place for carrying out espionage work. Everybody knew where everybody else was at a particular time, and suspicion would be roused by even a slight deviation from the norm.

The norm! Her existence had dwindled down to the narrow perimeters of a rock pile, and she was amazed at how quickly she had accepted those perimeters, fashioning her life around them. The frantic bustle of her Seattle office, even the peaceful ambience of her apartment there, were like some vaguely remembered dream. Jerry's face was a blurred outline in her memory, and she had ceased to wonder what his reaction was to her island incarceration. She was living a life apart, and every day her previous existence took on a more remote reality while Rock Island pressed more immediate tentacles round her.

It had been a world dominated by the violent see-saw of her emotions as inspired by Lyle

Hemming. At one moment she succumbed to the dream of loving him and being loved in return; the next, there was an upsurge of angry hate when he became the man she had despised for so many years. . . .

'Hey, green eyes!'

Sally started out of her reverie, registering with a faint inner smile that Tim had used her own formula for identifying him on herself. She let the smile surface as she looked across the table at him. 'What did I do?'

'It's what you didn't do,' he grumbled good-naturedly. 'It's hard to win this game when your partner's nine-tenths in another world! Do you know what you just played?'

Her eyes fell on the topmost card in the centre of the table, a two of spades, and went with a guilty flush to the king of the same suit in her hand. 'Oh, I'm sorry, Tim,' she gasped.

'It's okay, but try to drag your mind away from the white dress and orange blossom, will you?'

The game proceeded, and Sally made a valiant effort to concentrate on the cards in her hand, but a vision of what must have been a mediocre forties romantic movie kept flashing across her mind. In that kind of scenario, she would have floated down some familiar church aisle on the arm of her proud father, heavy white satin falling chastely to do no more than suggest her slender curves, a veil of billowing tulle making drama of her eyes and hair. And at the end of the aisle a man waited for her in the traditional way . . . Lyle. Of course.

Tim's irritated indrawn breath drew her back to the game in progress, and for the rest of the evening

she was a model partner, playing the right cards at
the right time. Romantic dreams had no reality for
her at that moment; in fact, it was laughable that
she had even entertained the thought that Lyle
would ever participate in that kind of wedding. A
writer of popular fiction would more likely go for
a quick civil wedding, dispensing with the traditional hearts and flowers. It was a moot point
anyway. No wedding would ever take place between Sally Brown and Lyle Hemming ... it
wasn't, and never had been, in the cards.

The solution of her quandary as to how to spend
some time in the assistant's cottage came with
remarkable ease the following evening. Dinner was
simmering slowly in the oven when the Captain
came into the kitchen.

'Look, honey, I can keep an eye on things here
if you want to go tidy up a little for Lyle.'

'Tidy up?' she asked, puzzled.

'Well,' he disparaged, 'I know men on their own
are notorious for not giving a damn about their
surroundings, but somehow I think Lyle would
appreciate having his bed changed and his floor
swept once in a while.'

Understanding lit her eyes, and at that moment
she wasn't concerned with the chauvinistic policy
behind his words. Captain Bradshaw came from
the old school, where men provided the living and
women provided the living comforts. From anyone
else, Sally might have resented it, but the Captain
was a dear, old-fashioned man. Besides, she would
have a ready-made excuse for visiting the small
cottage while its owner was absent performing the

most prolonged duty of the day when he made verbal reports on prevailing conditions.

Armed with fresh sheets from the upstairs linen cupboard, Sally made her legitimate way to the cottage, ignoring the sneaking feeling that what she intended to do was underhanded, unethical. The taxpayers of the State of Washington were providing the means to carry on an English Department in their university, and surely they had a right to know what one of their English professors produced in his spare time.

Warmth greeted her as she let herself into the cottage and closed the door behind her. The room, as she had expected it would be, was immaculately neat and tidy, a tribute to the man who occupied it. Even the bed was made up, not a wrinkle showing on its cotton tapestry bedcover. Sally walked over to it and dropped the clean linen at the foot of the bed before indulging the curiosity that drew her eyes like a magnet to the table under the window.

The typewriter looked efficiently bare as her feet took her towards it, the table neat except for a brown manilla folder enclosing a sizeable manuscript. Her hands rested first on the barren lines of the typewriter, then moved to touch the cool hardness of the manuscript's cover. Was there really this much work in one novel of detective fiction? she wondered as she dipped her head sideways to assess the pile of typed sheets. Conscience rose up and smote her as her fingers ran down the edge of the top cover. A writer's work was sacrosanct until it reached the buying public through its various agents.

But did Lyle Hemming deserve that kind of consideration when he was producing work of an inferior quality? Did he deserve the sinecure of a university appointment when, unknown to his students, he was producing work he was ashamed to acknowledge publicly?

Sally's fingers tensed on the cover and slowly lifted it. The job of a journalist was to expose people who pretended to be what they were not, and Lyle was a prime example of that philosophy.

The Silken Thread. The title flashed over her blinking eyes before they went down to the author's name in small type. Lyle Hemming. Not John Ainslie. A confused clamour started somewhere inside Sally. Was it possible she had been wrong? That Lyle was a *bona fide* author in the best sense of the word? Her fingers seemed frozen to the edge of the page as she stared down at the title. *The Silken Thread.* It was a title that could indicate any kind of book ... mystery, intrigue, romance. ...

Sally's fingers trembled as they separated the title page from the next one down. A dedication page. Only a few words were typed in the middle of it, but they were words that seared painfully into her brain, words she would never forget.

'For My Wife, Rosalie.'

Wife ... wife ... Rosalie ... Rosalie. ...

Sickness churned acidly inside her, the significance of those few words only gradually bearing in on her. Hysteria rose like a bubble in her throat, expelling itself in a strangled cry of pain. There had never been any possibility of that white dress and orange blossom wedding, she thought disjointedly. He was married ... Lyle was married already to a woman called Rosalie. One he loved, because he had dedicated his book to her. Pain twisted inside Sally, a wringing pain that squeezed her life's blood and left it pallid. He had never loved her, Sally Brown. She had been a stopgap in life's way-station for him. Like the college girls who fawned at his feet.

Her spine seemed permanently crooked as she ran to the door and wrenched it open, her eyes reaching up to the flashing light from the tower. It was like a bland symbol of the man himself, offering an impartial glow to every creature in its orbit. Sobbing, she stumbled back in the dimming light to the main house.

She had been one of those creatures, offering her heart without condition to a man already possessed of a wife . . . a wife he loved. How he must have laughed at his easy conquest of a girl with her supposedly sophisticated background! Laughed like a maniac inside when she had confided her lack of experience with men. Had he believed that? Probably not, but did it matter? Did anything matter now except that she should get off this god-forsaken island and back to the life she was familiar with?

Stopping only to shuck off her boots in the narrow hall, she ran upstairs without glancing into the sitting room and slammed her door behind her. Still in her jacket, she sat down at the side of the bed closest to the small window, the squared panes blurring as she looked out sightlessly at the leaden sky. The tears were more of anger than anything else, a deep slow-burning anger that mounted into an icy fury totally alien to her nature. Her head

swung round sharply to the door when there was a
tentative tap on it, and she was relieved to hear
Captain Bradshaw's deep-toned voice. She couldn't
have borne to face Lyle Hemming at that moment;
she would have wanted to scratch his eyes out,
punch the cynical expression from his face.

'Sally? You all right?'

Her muffled, 'Yes,' must have alarmed him, because he turned the handle and peered cautiously
round the door. He might have been her father
coming to her bedroom at home to smooth her
ruffled teenage feathers, and she forced a smile for
his benefit.

'You're sure? You weren't gone long enough to
do much over at the cottage, so I wondered. . . .'

Sally smoothed back her hair with both hands,
then quickly stroked away the tears under her eyes.
'Lyle's a very self-contained man,' she smiled tautly
with her mouth, leaving her eyes a sea-washed
green. 'He has great housekeeping skills.'

'Well, I guess you could expect that, seeing he
was brought up here.' He paused, hesitating yet
obviously wanting to say something else. 'If there's
anything bothering you, you could—talk to me.
Maybe I can't solve your problems, but it helps to
have somebody to talk to at times.'

Sally's head dropped forward and she studied
her white-socked feet intently, her hair falling like
a curtain round her face. She shook her head
finally. 'No—thanks. I guess I just—felt homesick
all of a sudden.'

'You shouldn't be like that when you're with
your fiancé,' he probed quietly, 'not if your home's
going to be with him for the rest of your life.'

'I—don't think I'll be spending the rest of my life with Lyle Hemming,' she burst out, unable to resist the relief of confiding in this man who reminded her so much of her father.

The Captain gave a soft exclamation. 'Is it because of us being here?'

'You and Tim? No,' she shook her head again, 'in fact, I'm very glad you—came when you did.' Or my precious virtue would have been just another memory, she added silently, bitterly.

'Were you really engaged to him?' He came and sat at the foot of the bed, his far-seeing eyes compassionate.

'No,' she sighed. 'I thought so, but—well, it's not possible now. I really don't want to talk about it any more, Captain,' she appealed, a catch in her voice.

'Whatever you like,' he said heavily, getting up and looking down at her bent head. 'But I hope you'll work things out, because you're both fine people and as an onlooker, I think you seem suited to each other.'

Sally looked up, her eyes growing hard. 'No. No, we're not suited in any way, Captain. But thanks anyway.' He patted her shoulder, turning away to the door, when she tagged on, 'Captain Bradshaw, you won't—mention anything about this to L-Lyle, will you?'

'Of course not,' he assured her gruffly. 'Even if I wanted to, I doubt if he'd let me. He's a good man, but he's very reserved about his private life—and that's his privilege, of course.' He gave her a half salute and went out.

Reserved! She supposed that was a word to de-

scribe his neglecting to mention the small fact that
he already had a wife when he asked her to marry
him. Was that his line with every girl foolish
enough to fall for him? She got up wearily and
walked to the window, sliding her jacket off and
throwing it back on the bed.

Night was already on its way, its darkness mingl-
ing with the grey clouds to shed a half-gloom over
the moss-covered rocks. How had Lyle managed
to keep his wife hidden all these years? There had
never been a whisper about a wife's existence round
the campus, a remarkable feat of sleight of hand
on Lyle's part, he who loved to eat his cake and
keep it too. Where was she now, this wife? If he
loved her, as his book's dedication seemed to indicate, why hadn't she shared this exile with him?
Maybe she didn't love him enough to spend
months incarcerated on Rock Island, maybe. . . .

Angry with herself, Sally shook off the questions
that were filling her mind to the exclusion of all
else. What could it possibly matter, now, whether
his wife—Rosalie—was blonde or brunette,
sophisticated or shyly retiring? Her existence was
enough.

Sally toyed with the idea of pleading illness and
staying in her room, but pride prevailed over the
subterfuge and she rinsed her face and combed her
hair before going downstairs to carry on with
supper preparations.

Thanks to the Captain's efforts in that direction,
there was little else to do apart from serving the
meal and calling the men in from the sitting room.
Her eyes avoided direct contact with Lyle's and,

although she sensed a faintly puzzled pair of eyes on her back, he followed her with the others and took his place at the table. Her eyes on her plate, she sent up a small prayer of thanks that relations had been far from cordial between them for the past day or two. He would see nothing strange in her coolness towards him, and that was a lot better than a face-to-face confrontation. All she wanted to do was to get off the island and resume her own tranquil life. She looked up startled when Lyle made an announcement, his eyes watchfully on hers.

'Good news, folks. The weather's clearing, so it shouldn't be too much longer till you get back to civilisation.'

A lump rose in Sally's throat, and she whispered past it, 'When?'

His jaw tensed at the urgency of that one word, and he looked down at his meal as he said quietly, 'Maybe as early as tomorrow afternoon.' The yellow-brown eyes came up again suddenly, an expression she couldn't interpret lurking in their depths. 'Sounds as if you'll be glad to shake Rock Island'—and me, his eyes added silently—'from your heels.'

'Don't forget I have a job to go back to.' From near muteness, Sally erupted in a spate of chatter. 'Heavens, I've been here this long, and I haven't taken one picture yet for my article. Maybe I can shoot some tomorrow before the boat gets here. Will your brother and his wife be on it?'

'Yes.'

'Good, then I'll be able to interview them, won't I?'

'In passing,' he said cryptically, 'while they're getting off the boat and you're getting on it.'

'Well, I'll sure as hell be glad to get off this heap of rock,' Tim waxed enthusiastic, his blue eyes belatedly apologetic as he looked at Lyle and Sally. 'Not that I don't appreciate all that you two have done, but it drives me crazy not being able to get up and go.'

No one saw fit, in the ensuing pause, to remind him that the other crew members of the ill-fated boat would never get up and go again. The immediate moment was one for rejoicing in their release.

'What are you going to do, Captain?' Sally broke the silence her voice brittle.

'Go home first,' he said quietly, 'then pay a few calls.'

Her hand moved of its own accord to lie over his on the table and squeeze it understandingly. It was her left hand, the bandage growing grubby over the wound.

'How's your hand?' Lyle asked, as if reminded by her automatic gesture.

'My hand? Oh, it's fine. In fact, I've almost forgotten about it.' It was the truth, she realised as she turned surprised eyes on it. She had learned to compensate for the awkwardness, and it no longer hurt.

'Still, I'd better have a look at it later on,' Lyle stated so positively that panic seized her. How could she bear his touch, the fingers that could be so gentle when the occasion called for it? Occasions like caressing her body to a passionate response as well as caring for her hand.

'No,' she refused quickly, blinking as she looked away from the level stare of his eyes. 'I can have it seen to in Seattle.'

'I'm sure you can, but I'd still like to take a look at it myself,' he came back unequivocally, and Sally decided to let it drop. She could find some excuse for dodging his attention later on.

The dishes were soon disposed of in the general air of celebration among the three reluctant exiles, and when Lyle came back from his evening chore they played cards for one last time, the companionship sweeter for that reason. Coffee was replaced by brandy for Lyle and the Captain, beer for Tim, and white wine for Sally. Perversely, because she wanted to keep a clear head, the semi-sweet wine affected her in a way it never had before. Maybe that was because she had never tried to drown her emotions before, to dull the pain that rose to grind in her chest as the evening went on, a pain she made worse by letting her eyes stray to the long sensitive fingers that shuffled and dealt the cards when it was Lyle's turn to do so. More than once their eyes met, his levelly steady as if he knew every thought that strayed into her mind.

Finally she rose, not finding it difficult to simulate a yawn. 'Well, that's it for me, fellers, I'm going to bed. But don't let me stop you from playing whatever you want, the noise won't bother me.'

She moved with unaccustomed unsteadiness to the door, her feet slowing when Lyle said from behind, 'Don't go yet, Sally, I want to look at your hand.'

'It's fine,' she waggled it in demonstration, 'really.'

'Well, you two can argue it out,' the Captain put in traitorously, getting to his feet and punching Tim on the arm. 'We've got an exciting day ahead of us, and I want to appreciate every minute of it.'

'What——?' Tim looked up at him, bewildered, and then recognition dawned. 'Oh, yes, sure. I'm with you, Captain.'

Sally's feet seemed rooted to the spot as they filed past her, the Captain giving her a con-spiratorial wink in answer to her reproachful stare.

It was quiet in the kitchen when the two seamen had gone, silent in an oppressive way, unspoken words heavy in the air. Sally's senses swam in frightened circles, her leaden limbs forcing her to remain where she didn't want to be . . . in the same room with Lyle Hemming. As in a dream, she heard his chair scrape back, his voice quiet yet seeming to shatter the silence between them.

'Well?'

He wasn't asking about her hand, wanting to see it . . . there was a world of meaning in that one word, a meaning she couldn't—wouldn't—face. She held out the offending hand.

'Well?'

CHAPTER EIGHT

LYLE came to her, taking her hand in both of his but making no effort to examine its state of health. Instead, his eyes scrutinised hers with a quiet intensity that unnerved her. Blinking, she told herself that she must be imagining the stark hurt lingering in their depths as though they were only the tip of an iceberg she could only guess at.

She drew a deep ragged breath. He was ruthless when it came to man–woman relationships, that was something she had to remember. If only . . . her eyes dropped to where his long fingers cradled her hand, gently, so gently. Even that slight touch had the power to send awareness tingling along her nerve ends, shocking in its intensity yet curiously numbing the censor pulsing in her brain.

'What's happened, Sally?' The resonance of his voice hit an answering chord somewhere within her, and her head tilted back so that his leanly planed face came starkly into her view. 'Didn't we start to love each other?'

Love . . . yes, she had thought that what was between them was love. For her, it had been . . . but not for him. How could it be when the fair Rosalie—and with a name like that, how could she be anything other than long, blonde, enchanting?—held prime place in his heart?

'No,' she corrected, solemnly sober when her mind was floating in the cushioned alcohol of the white wine she had consumed. 'I thought I loved you, but you. . . .'

Lyle loosed her hand with a smothered oath and drew her to him instead, his chin creating warmth against her skin when it grazed her cheek. 'You doubted me, when I——? Oh God, Sally, don't you know what you do to me?' His head rose and he stared down at her, his eyes feverish as they roamed the contours of her face. The flat palms of his hands went in a sliding motion down to the curving rise of her hips and pressed her to the hardness in his thighs, a movement more eloquently provocative than any number of words would have been.

'But, I—Lyle. . . .' she whispered throatily, cool reason deserting her as waves of heady sensation swept her and left her breathless. 'You're——' She had been about to remind him that he was married, to a woman he loved, but emotions that were purely physical ran like a flash flood through her resistance and left her clinging to the hard male potency of his thrusting body. His mouth touched and held hard to hers, provoking sensations that were more akin to drowning than loving him.

Trembling, her arms slid round his shoulders, her body moulding itself to the fevered hardness of his, parting only slightly to allow the slide of his fingers up over her ribcage under the thick wool of her sweater to the ready peaks that awaited his sensuous strokes.

His mouth teased and pressed and seemed one with hers as he lowered her to the floor and lay over her, grinding her spine against the cold hardness of the vinyl. Sally seemed suspended, as her body was, between cold, hard reality and the warm fantasy of Lyle making vibrant love to her.

His eyes looked heavy, their lids drooping, when
he pulled back briefly, and then his head dipped
lower, drawing shivering moans from her when he
directed his lips to the throbbing rise of her breasts,
inciting the wildness of a desire that pushed aside
every scruple she had fastidiously fostered. Nothing
mattered but the pounding needs that made mockery of the mild reaching towards fulfilment that
she had known before. Her lips parted and she
kissed him back, her mouth feeling like velvet
where his rough skin touched.

Love . . . yes, she loved him with every long-for-
gotten yearning, every girlish dream she had ever
cherished. Her hips moulded themselves to his, her
hands insistently caressing as she raised his head to
hers again and pulled it down to the eager wanting
in her lips that she made no effort to conceal. Love
. . . oh, God, how she loved him!

And didn't he love her, too? His breath laboured
harshly at her mouth, his body tensed to the height
of the same desire that rode roughshod over her. It
seemed so very natural when his fingers fumbled
momentarily with her jeans and then ran the zipper
smoothly down before easing them from her hips.
Yes, he loved her, needed her, wanted her as she
wanted him. His warmth covered her again, shocking her with its lustful nakedness, sobering her to
the reality she had pushed from her. Lyle didn't
love her; it was . . . it was . . . Rosalie he loved. His
wife . . . WIFE . . . the word materialised in high
letters in her mind's eye, and like a douse of ice
water cooled her ardour.

'No! No, Lyle! Let me go!'

'What?' his voice came dazedly from somewhere close above her. 'What did you say?'

The emotion-numbing wine fumes dissipated suddenly, devastatingly, and Sally heaved with all her might against the hard pinion of his body. 'Let me go,' she gasped, fighting for air as she pushed against his muscled shoulders and felt him give suddenly. 'I don't want this . . . please, just let me up!'

Whether it was her frantic plea, or his unwillingness to force a point he must have felt was already proved, but Lyle lifted from her, the yellow in his eyes dominant as he stared down at her. The curling brown of his chest hair rose in unison with his bare muscled stomach, fighting for a control Sally sought for in her own tortured body.

'Get up,' he said harshly, standing aside as she got tremulously to her feet before bending stiffly to pull on the clothes he had abandoned minutes before. 'There's a word—in fact, quite a few—for women like you. Come on, but don't come on'. She flinched when he uttered a potent oath as she rose, trembling, and pulled on her clothes, gathering them up from where he had cast them. 'You make me sick, women like you,' he castigated, his eyes flailing her round curves and narrow hips as she tremblingly pulled her clothing over them.

'Lyle, I . . . please, don't. . . .' She was begging, without knowing what she pleaded for. Shame lifted its warm red glow to her face as she fumbled, far less expertly than he had, at the zipper enclosing her jeans. She *had* led him on to expect more than she had delivered. A lot more, she thought dully, than she had ever offered to a man. Pain pressed an ache behind her eyes as she stumbled from the room and left Lyle's contemptuous eyes behind.

Although the headache grew worse after she had crept miserably into bed, she seemed not to have the energy to do anything about it. Instead she lay dry-eyed looking up at the ceiling, flinching when she heard the subdued bang of the door behind Lyle as he went out, her brain automatically counting the things she would never experience again after this night. The reflected glow faintly illuminating her room as the tower light revolved ceaselessly, the restless churning of the sea against the rocks, the excitement morning would bring. . . . Her pupils dilated in surprise. Excitement? On a desolate pile of rocks in the middle of nowhere?

She turned on her side and pulled the covers up over her ear. But her thoughts went on relentlessly. Each new day *had* brought the excitement of Lyle's company, sparking her veins to vibrant life even when relations weren't good between them. It was that she would miss most of all.

Why had she had to find out about his marriage?

The morning was more like April than December, Sally reflected as she went downstairs hours later. Incredible that grey sky had given way in hours to deepest blue, that white puffy clouds had replaced the leaden density of the past week.

It was early yet, but the eye that had become practised noted that the fire had been built up, the sitting room tidied, coffee keeping warm on the stove. She carried a cup to the table and sat down, carefully avoiding the area where she had lain with

Lyle the night before.

Although there were no signs of it, he had probably had breakfast. It still amazed her that, even in these days of sex liberation, he was more meticulous than the most houseproud woman. Did Rosalie find that hard to live with? Or was she ultra-liberated herself? They must have the kind of marriage that made no dependent demands on each other, both of them living their lives like single people who happened to be married. Yet Sally couldn't really believe that that was the kind of life to satisfy Lyle. He was too alive to the physical demands of his maleness, he needed the fulfilment women provided.

And that, she sighed, was the crux of the whole matter. He had become accustomed to looking elsewhere when normally married people would find fulfilment in each other.

'Well, isn't this a great morning?'

She started and turned, not having heard the Captain come downstairs. Forcing a smile, she got up and went to the coffee pot. 'It certainly is if it means we can get off this place today.' She handed the mug to him, then added to her own cup before sitting down opposite. He looked across at her sadly.

'You're still anxious to get away?'

'Of course. Why wouldn't I be?'

He shrugged and sipped at his coffee. 'I just thought that—well, I thought maybe you and Lyle worked out your differences last night after we left.'

'Some differences can't be worked out,' Sally said in a crisp way that put an end to that branch of the conversation, and the Captain sighed as he looked down into his mug. Forcing brightness, she added, 'Would you believe that I've been here for a week and now I'm going to be in a rush to do the work I came here for? The light's really good for taking pictures this morning, and I have to catch up on my notes.'

'Did you do the recordings this morning?' he asked from under the shaggy grey of his brows, and Sally frowned. How could she have forgotten that essential chore?

'No, I—I guess Lyle did it, he was around early this morning. His book's finished,' she tacked on defensively. 'I only agreed to do it while he worked on that.'

'It must be quite something to finish writing a book,' the Captain meditated. 'We should have celebrated that last night too.'

Yes, they should have, Sally realised belatedly, then felt a sour taste rise in her throat. Celebrate what?—Lyle's book dedicated to a wife who apparently treated him as if he didn't exist?

'He'll probably have a party when he gets back to Seattle,' she proffered, closing her lips round the words.

'Is he leaving when we do? He came here to write the book, and now it's finished——'

'I've no idea,' Sally bit off churlishly, then, guilty because it wasn't the dear old Captain's fault that her love life was such a mess, she hastily made amends. Getting up, she smiled and said lightly, 'I'll make us some breakfast. Tim can fend for himself when he gets down.'

While she was busy at the stove, her mind ran in

its now accustomed groove. It hadn't occurred to her that Lyle might leave with them, but it was entirely likely. The book, his reason for being here, was finished. He had no reason to remain on Rock Island.

How wrong that assumption was she found out later that morning when, complete with camera and lenses, she made her way up into the tower, her aim to take flash pictures of the working heart of the lighthouse, the machinery that recorded wind and weather on this outer bastion of the coastguard service.

She drew back when Lyle swung round from the machines and looked coldly at her. Despite herself, her eyes went hungrily over the faint blue of his cleanshaven chin, the neatly brushed hair, and lastly to the eyes that offered a cold welcome.

'Did you want something?' he asked coolly—insultingly, she leapt to conclude, in view of the work she had done here during the past week.

'I just wanted to make sure you were—seeing to things up here.'

His hand gave a mocking sweep round the glistening machines. 'As you see, I'm managing without your able help.' His eyes went obviously to the camera slung across her shoulder. 'Was there something else you wanted?'

Her fingers tightened round the camera strap, but she managed a level-sounding, 'Yes, there is. I need some pictures for my article, and——'

'Fine,' he interrupted, striking a dramatic pose against the machinery, his eyes like flint as they stared into hers. 'Will this do?'

She hadn't wanted pictures including him, but

the objection died in her throat. Her article would have more immediacy with a human element. Besides, she didn't want him thinking that it meant anything to her one way or the other if he appeared in living colour in her layout. He held the pose while she readied the camera, the hardness in his features unrelenting even when bulbs flashed in his eyes. Sparing time to be vicious as her finger clicked the shutter, she sent up a silent prayer that none of the pictures would be usable when the moment of truth came, even though her reputation as a photo-journalist would suffer by it.

'Thanks,' she said briefly when it was over, going to the spiral stairs and looking back at his still figure to ask conversationally, 'Are you coming back to Seattle with us?'

'Did you want me to?' he parried instantly, nothing in his voice indicating whether he cared if she did or not.

'No,' she said shortly, and began her descent.

'You're spending Christmas with your family?' he asked unexpectedly, and she stopped, swivelling round to look at him again.

'Yes, of course.'

'I'm doing the same.'

'You're not spending it with your——?' She broke off abruptly, knowing she couldn't articulate 'wife' without betraying the agony that word had wrought over the past twelve hours. 'With your friends?' she substituted.

'No, I'm not.'

'Oh.' Her hand slid and then gripped on the rail, her hair falling silkily beside her face when she looked down into the spiral. 'Well, I'd better go and get my things together if the boat's coming soon.'

She hesitated, waiting to hear him speak again, a wild hope surging somewhere in the soft depths of her. He wasn't spending the holidays with the obvious person for a married man ... did that mean that the split between him and Rosalie was something final, irrevocable?

Lyle said nothing, so she continued down the circling stairs, her light steps reflecting the hope that tapped its tattoo in her breast. Rosalie meant nothing to him ... marriage could be dissolved almost as easily as it was contracted ... why had she been such a fool as not to know that and act accordingly? She stopped at the lowest level and looked up, a smile tentatively touching her lips. Oh, Lyle, she thought tremulously, why didn't you tell me? All I wanted to know was that you loved me, not the wife who was more out of your life than in it. Had he wanted her to prove her love before telling her about the wife who was unimportant to him? He didn't know that Sally knew of his wife's existence. Didn't know that she had stolen an illicit look at his manuscript, the one. . . .

Her feet retracted the few upward steps she had taken and she stumbled blindly to the bottom and let herself out of the tower, the slight breeze lifting the ends of her hair in a sighing motion. Her hand lifted to press against her eyes, but Lyle's dedication of the book he had just written rose starkly behind her hand ... *For My Wife, Rosalie.* Whatever the reason for their apartness, Lyle still loved her.

Emotion heaved and made rags of her nerves as

she stood there immobile, her hand still covering her eyes. When at last it fell to her side and she moved off across the cushioned rocks, her mouth had firmed into a new line of hardness. So she had been burned, as many women had been burned before by Lyle Hemming, and would be again. It was a salutory experience, one Sally Brown would never repeat.

The unnatural calm that obviously bothered Captain Bradshaw remained with her for the rest of the morning and extended into the early afternoon when the supply boat came, bringing with it John Hemming and his wife Verna. As Lyle had forecast, their meeting was brief, and she had just a jumbled impression of a man not quite as tall as Lyle but with unmistakable resemblance in features, and a vivacious dark-haired woman who would obviously have liked to quiz Sally about her stay on Rock Island as they briefly clasped hands.

'Did Lyle take good care of you?' she called as Sally stepped on to the precariously rocking vessel.

'Yes,' she called back, turning to look back at the couple watching her from the wooden dock, her eyes drawn upwards then to the solitary figure outlined against the sky at the top of the rocks. 'He took good care of me.' And left my life cold and without hope in the process, she added silently, a mist that had nothing to do with the spray fanning out from the razor rocks surrounding the landing stage.

'You'll find yourself quite a heroine when you get back to Seattle!' Verna shouted as the engine spluttered into new life and the boat began its thrust through the whitecapped swell reaching hungrily towards the island. 'Lyle told us how——'

The rest of her words were lost as the boat made headway from the island, but Sally wasn't interested in hearing whatever Lyle had told his brother over the radio-telephone. One thing she knew for sure. He had not reported, among the weather data, his almost success in seducing one Sally Brown.

Somehow her own apartment seemed small, cramped—and that was ridiculous, Sally told herself when she crossed to the galley kitchen off the living room and ran water into the kettle. What could be more confining than a lump of rock in the middle of an angry sea? Yet the illusion persisted as she went into the bedroom and donned a silk robe after removing the jeans and loose sweater she had worn all day.

Seated in her favourite chair close to the living room window, she ignored the instant coffee at her elbow and leaned her head back against the pale green upholstery.

Verna Hemming hadn't been joking about Sally finding herself a heroine on her arrival back in Seattle. Reporters from the dailies, as well as local television cameras, had trained their attention on the survivors of an enforced exile on Rock Island. Most of the coverage had been concentrated on Captain Bradshaw and Tim Nielsen, and she had been separated from them within minutes of landing at the pier.

She glanced at her watch and saw that it was almost time for the six o'clock news. Getting up, she crossed to the television and switched it on, hearing and ignoring reports of guerilla warfare in distant parts of the world. Selfishly, her own misery seemed far more important at that moment. She heard the beginning of the local news, glancing idly at the screen while she sipped her coffe. A threatened strike of schoolteachers, a fire at a nursing home where, miraculously, none of the elderly residents had lost their lives.

Her attention sharpened when a different scene flashed on the screen, her own face looking strangely different as it stared into the camera, her eyes enormous between the tangled weave of her hair, tossed by the biting winds that had pursued them all the way from Rock Island. Her voice seemed unreal as she answered the reporter's questions.

'What was it like being marooned on a lighthouse for a whole week, Sally?'

'I understand your only companion for the week was Professor Hemming of our own university. How did you feel about that?'

'You went to get background information on an article you're doing for the magazine you work for—*Northwest Then and Now*—so how come you were able to take over the running of the lighthouse?'

'You just did a little to help out, so that Professor Hemming could get on with the work he went there to do? Was he writing a thesis of some kind?'

Her stumbling answers were mercifully cut off when the cameras swivelled to the Captain and Tim Nielsen, looking more true to themselves than she had. Captain Bradshaw was brusquely uninformative, except that his grief over the loss of his crew was obviously moving. Tim, his arm round a redhaired woman who had come to meet him, flashed his confident grin and said this was the happiest moment in his life.

Sally got up and went to turn off the set, halting to stand in frozen silence when the enthusiastic announcer came back on camera to say roguishly, 'It's been brought to my attention that Professor Hemming didn't go to Rock Island, where his brother John is the permanent keeper, to write a dry, dusty thesis! But you'll find out all about the Professor's hidden literary life when you read Sally Brown's article in *Northwest Then and Now*! And now, I'll return you to our studio.'

The voice that followed immediately was a meaningless jumble of sound, and Sally leaned down with stiff fingers to switch off the set. Oh God, she thought, stumbling back to her chair and huddling down into it as if surrounded by nameless phantoms. What had Tim told them? It had to be Tim, the Captain was discretion itself. The scene in the main house sitting room rose accusingly in her mind . . . the scene where she had divulged her suspicions as to Lyle's literary identity, when she had thought he was John Ainslie, the successful producer of detective fiction. Why hadn't she corrected the misapprehension when she had found out that Lyle had written the book under his own name?

Her fingers clutched at the throat of her robe in a convulsive clasp that whitened her knuckles. Lyle would think that it was she, not Tim, who had made public his writing endeavours. She, who had castigated him for producing literature for the masses! Writhing inside, she visualised the hard clench of his lean jaw, the flinty hardness of his eyes. He would never believe, in a million years, that she——

She straightened suddenly, her hair brushing the high back of the chair. There was no television on Rock Island, so Lyle wouldn't see the broadcast. He would never know of the announcer's titillating statement, the words which could, apparently, have come from her.

Yet that too, she decided, leaving the chair to listlessly inspect the contents of the refrigerator, had a quality of hurt. He had made it only too clear that she had interested him in a purely temporary fashion, that he would, in the end, go back to Rosalie . . . his wife.

'You're getting to be quite a camerawoman,' Dave joked as he dropped a pile of glossies on her desk two weeks later. 'What are you trying to do, take my job?'

'Hardly.' Sally's fingers lingered on the edge of the photographic pile, wanting yet not wanting to see the results of her camera work on Rock Island.

She had done her best to put Lyle from her thoughts, and had succeeded in a numbed way during the daytime when work and holiday celebrations had pushed the hurt aside. It was the nights that tormented her, lying sleepless on her own bed or in the room that had been hers in her parents' house while Christmas was celebrated. Her mother, despite her absorption in a creative world that necessarily excluded, to a certain extent, the pull of family ties, noticed the shadows smudged beneath her eyes and commented on her daughter's unusual lack of verve.

'There must be a man in your life,' she said in the kitchen on the day after Christmas when they were alone. Her eyes had reflected a concern that was purely maternal, and Sally had wanted to grasp that rare moment of intimacy with a mother whose life was normally lived on a different plane from her own, but her father had come in them.

'How about coming out with me to blow the cobwebs away?' he had proposed to the daughter who had, in the past, accompanied him on many such trips. With a pang, Sally looked back at her mother before agreeing. There might have been a moment of woman-to-woman understanding, an experienced shoulder to lean on, but she let the moment slip. What did her mother know about a hopeless love without promise of fulfilment? Her own love had been free and clear, without the problems that beset Sally's love life. Oh, she would care, but she wouldn't really understand her daughter's love for a man who was already committed to the reality of his wife.

So she went sailing with her father, and the next day Jerry came to collect her and drive her back to town. He had stayed to lunch, and it was only later, when she sat silently beside him as he drove with concentrated attention along the freeway, that she allowed herself to feel the surprise her mother's parting words had caused.

'He's not the one, is he?' Stella whispered at her ear as she hugged her daughter beside the car.

Not the one . . . no, Jerry could never be the one who made her blood quicken to send its golden glow through her veins. Would any man, ever?

Sally came to with an abrupt shock, feeling the sharp edges of the pictures Dave had developed against her pressing fingers. Slowly, reluctantly, she looked down at the first of the glossy images, breathing a sigh of relief and even smiling slightly when she saw Tim's impudent grin, the Captain's sober face outlined against the sturdy background of the main house. There were others, and she flipped quickly through them, the hurt of dear familiarity solidifying when the last few pictures opened to her view.

Dave was right, they were excellent shots. Every detail of the room at the heart of the tower's operation stood out in sharp relief. Including Lyle ... her gaze started slowly and then went with hungry speed over every detail of his lean features. Even the tawny brown of his eyes seemed to leap from the shiny print and look mockingly into hers. But he hadn't only mocked her that morning ... he had been coldly, blindly angry.

She sighed, shuffling the pictures together and laying them to one side. Shouldn't she have been the one to feel anger? Lyle had changed her whole life by asking her to marry him; it had fallen back into familiar but different lines when she knew about Rosalie. Was it her pride that had hurt most, crumbling to dust when she realised that Lyle had sought to make use of her, to treat her as he had so many others as a stopgap for the wife he loved?

Determination firmed her chin. To hell with Lyle Hemming and every other insensitive boor like him! Who needed him?

CHAPTER NINE

'YOU did such a fantastic job on that article about the Governor,' Jerry enthused, the sleeve of his beige-coloured suit brushing against the file tray as he sat on Sally's desk and beamed down at her, 'he wants you to do a piece on every Governor the State has ever had! What do you think?'

Sally shrugged, obviously disappointing him with her lack of vibrant enthusiasm. 'All right, if that's what you want me to do.'

'You know what I want you to do,' Jerry said darkly after a pause when his eyes rested thoughtfully on the clear green of hers. 'What's happened to you, Sally?' he asked quietly. 'You haven't been the same since Christmas—in fact, you haven't been the same since you went on that wild goose chase to Rock Island.'

Sally's head jerked up defensively. 'We've had good response to the lighthouse article,' she pointed out acidly.

'I know, I know. You're a damn good writer, that's obvious from the Governor's request that you do more.' He hesitated. 'I wasn't talking about your professional dedication. You seem to have gone away from me since you went on that damned lighthouse project.'

'I wasn't aware that I'd been with you before that,' Sally said crisply, ignoring his scowl as the office intercom buzzed. She looked up at him.

'There's a call for you from Jetstar Industries, do
you want to take it here?'

All personal cares were erased from his brow as
he jumped to his feet and said, 'No, I'll take it in
my office, I have the advertising figures there.'

Sally's eyes followed his departing figure as she
relayed the message to the switchboard, then she
sat back against her curved office chair and stared
sightlessly at the door Jerry had closed behind
him.

Time, the legendary healer, had stroked blurring
edges round the experiences of five months ago.
Sometimes it seemed incredible that she had spent
a week sequestered on Rock Island; on an occa-
sional night when she lay waiting for sleep, it
seemed only yesterday that Lyle had made love to
her on the kitchen floor of the main house. It was
at those times, no matter how often she told herself
the experience had been meaningless, that memory
rose to curse her. As if his every sinew and muscle
was carved in dear familiarity on her own flesh,
she felt again the wild, speechless excitement that
turned her limbs to water.

But those were what she had come to think of as
the bad nights. As winter gave way to the fresh
gold of daffodils, then the rounded pink and red of
rhododendron blossoms, hurt faded into a dull
ache that receded further with each passing day.
She was getting over Lyle. No longer was she alert,
when she wandered Seattle's streets, for the sight
of his spare, studious figure with its topping of
thick dark hair meticulously brushed over his well-
shaped head. Rock Island became a dream, recalled
only slightly in the daytime hours when she caught

sight of the faint scar of the axe wound between her thumb and forefinger.

Pete Jenson, a newcomer to the magazine, poked his head round the door, and Sally blinked, then responded automatically to the freckled grin he offered.

'Deep in thought?' he asked, still keeping a respectable distance.

Sally laughed. 'No, not really. Can I help you, Pete?'

It was strange, she mused wryly as Pete came and dropped into the chair opposite, how indifference to their charms made men all the keener to get through the barrier she had subtly erected round her emotions. Jerry never ceased his campaign to make himself important in her life, and Pete had made use of the two months he had been with the magazine to beat against the wall he only dimly perceived. Her eyes went over Pete's sand-coloured hair now and progressed to his smiling grey-blue eyes and wide, well-formed lips. Had Lyle spoiled her for every man on earth?

'You could, but you won't,' Pete smiled ruefully, sobering as he went on, 'Jerry's given me an assignment for next week's issue, and I want to pick your brains.'

'So go ahead.' Sally leaned back in her chair, flattered that Pete wanted to draw from her experience, small though it was.

'Well, there's a cocktail party tomorrow night to honour a local author, and I was wondering if you could give me a few pointers on the kind of questions I should ask him—it's a publicity thing, of course,' Pete said negligently, 'but I'd like to stand out among the other reporters there. I mean,' he waved an earnest hand, 'what they write is read today and forgotten tomorrow, but people *save* our magazine!'

Smiling, Sally lifted a yellow pencil from her desk and tossed it between her fingers. 'I doubt if too many people do that, Pete, in spite of what Jerry tells you, especially when the article's about a local who's written a few lines of poetry. But go ahead, tell me about it and I'll try to think of a few unusual questions to ask him—or her.'

Pete stared at her incredulously. 'Where have you been, Sally? This isn't some old lady who scribbles in her spare time! His book's a best-seller nationwide, book clubs and the whole bit.'

'This magazine,' she reminded him tartly, 'ties the past to the present, in case you've forgotten. There are lots of magazines who report on sudden successes—we don't.'

'This author has a past locally,' Pete insisted. 'In fact, you probably know him, since he teaches at your alma mater—Lyle Hemming, his name is.'

The pencil stilled, threatening to break between her white-knuckled fingers. Lyle . . . oh, God, Lyle! Why hadn't she known at once? Maybe she would have if she hadn't studiously avoided the literary reviews over the past months . . . not that she had ever imagined that Lyle would make headlines, but any talk of an author's work had served only as a painful reminder of an episode she would rather— *had* to—forget.

'I——' She felt faint, disorientated, but Pete's puzzled eyes made her aware of how odd her behaviour must seem to him. 'I—knew him, of course, though he wasn't my teacher.' Her ragged thoughts seemed about to slip from her control, and she moistened her lips, which suddenly seemed dry, with her tongue. 'Maybe you should—talk to his wife, if you want to do an in-depth piece on him.'

'Are you crazy?' Incredibly, Pete's astonishment grew. 'Don't you know that the book is *about* his wife? About how he married her just after he got his first teaching job somewhere in Oregon and then found out she had this incurable illness? He took care of her until she died three years later— Sally, are you okay?'

The pencil snapped between Sally's fingers, and she felt the colour drain from her cheeks. *He took care of her until she died.* The words roared and then receded in her ears, over and over again as she stared sightlessly at Pete's concerned face. Rosalie . . . oh, God, *Rosalie*. . . .

Sally drew back at the entrance to the hotel ballroom, the hum of conversation interspersed with polite laughter sending a note of panic shivering down her spine.

They were early, Pete had insisted on that when she had called him to ask if she could accompany him to the cocktail party in Lyle's honour. She had sensed his hesitation after hearing her request, and had assured him that the interview would be entirely his, she wanted to go as a spectator only. Something of her urgency must have got through to him, because he agreed with no further trouble.

Pete's stocky figure was at her side now as they

went past the door check and went into the elegantly arrayed ballroom, one of the smaller salons reserved for occasions like these. The urgency that had motivated her request had fled at the door, and she put her hand lightly on Pete's grey-suited sleeve.

'You go ahead and do your thing,' she half whispered above the chatter surrounding them, 'I'll fade into the woodwork.'

'There's no need to do that,' Pete started his protest, but Sally was already wending her way through the smiling groups to a far corner, her eyes darting to every man in the room who was approximately Lyle's height. A white-jacketed waiter held out a tray of cocktails and she absently took one, sipping it when she reached her hideaway, her eyes luminously green over it as she scanned the room, seeking yet dreading seeing the man she had come to see.

Suddenly it didn't seem that important any more. What chance would there be to speak with him—*apologise* to him—in this crush of people? Wouldn't it have been more sensible to seek him out privately, go to his apartment? But then he might have closed the door in her face, might have forgotten her existence even. Her pride couldn't stand that.

Could it stand being humiliated much more devastatingly here in public? Pride, she mocked herself silently, what sins had been committed in its name! She had been right, morally, to shun his lovemaking after discovering, as she thought, that he had a wife existing—Lyle should have told her about Rosalie. There hadn't been time, the nagging voice persisted, after the Captain and Tim's arrival on the island.

Her mistake had been in judging the man at gossip value, and in denigrating what she, in her ignorance, had dubbed his inferior literature. What would it have mattered if he *had* been John Ainslie, a writer who gave relaxing pleasure to millions? Lyle had accused her of being a snob, and she realised now that she had been that in a literary sense.

But Lyle's book had, as it happened, held much more than entertainment value. Reading it far into the night before, she had wept bitter tears for the man who had cared tenderly for his wife of three short years . . . Rosalie . . . knowing she was dying, making her life as rich as he could make it while she lived. Sally herself had felt some of that tenderness in caring for someone ill . . . hadn't she known it after the accident with the axe? Her eyes went involuntarily to the scar on her hand, misting.

When she raised her head again, Lyle was there. He must have come in by the side door near her and he stood, remotely confident, at the far side of a fronding palm at Sally's left. She stepped back automatically behind the concealing palm, her eyes wide with recognition and another emotion that made breathing difficult.

He looked magnificent, the only word to describe his dark good looks in a well-cut charcoal suit and pristine white shirt that contrasted with his weathered brown skin. Trembling, Sally's eyes went up over the lean features, familiar yet forbidding in their remoteness, watching him greedily until he turned to the blonde woman by his side and made a smiling remark. Magda! Oh God, could she ever have forgotten the brittle blonde who had been with him that night at the club? She seemed even more radiant tonight, answering Lyle's smile with a secretive one of her own.

'Had an accident, ma'am? Let me take that from you and give you another.'

Dazedly, Sally looked up into the impassive face of a waiter, then down to the glass whose stem had inexplicably broken between her fingers. Numbly, she relinquished the severed glass and accepted a brimming new one in its place.

'Th-thank you.'

Her eyes were drawn hypnotically back to where Lyle was, and found him surrounded by a coterie of reporters, Pete among them, parrying their questions with an aplomb many celebrities would envy. Sally was so close she could hear his deep-pitched voice, laughingly polite, answering the quickfire questions. She came out of her stupor long enough to hear Pete's contribution.

'I'm from *Northwest Then and Now*, Dr Hemming,' he introduced himself, 'and I'd like to know——'

'You're from where?'

Pete reiterated his credentials and Sally blinked nervously. It was only too obvious that Lyle remembered her, but also evident that he hated her with a venom that was obvious in the harshness of his voice. Pete's question faded into obscurity as she swayed on her slender heels, knowing she was about to faint yet knowing she couldn't. Not here, not now.

She took one step, another, and came up against

a barrier of bodies that refused to yield, faces that looked with polite amazement as a dark roaring filled her ears and her legs slid, slipped from under her. . . .

Sally came to and found herself in darkness, in motion, her body slumped in a cushioned car seat, the shadowy figure beside her remotely silent as he seemed to propel the car forward by effort of will alone. She struggled to straighten her sagging spine, and saw, in the flashing illumination of a street light, that it was Lyle.

'Where are you taking me?' she croaked, the stem of her neck feeling fragile as she turned her eyes outward to the unfamiliar outlines of a residential area.

'You'll find out soon.'

Painfully, she swivelled her head to look at his profile, fitfully lit by the street lamps flashing by. It looked as harsh as his voice had sounded.

'Lyle, let me out. I—I want to go home.'

'When I'm good and ready to let you go,' he returned savagely, both hands manipulating the wheel as he turned into the parking area of a well-lit apartment building.

Sally seemed boneless when he pulled to a halt and came round to half-lift her from the passenger seat, the silk champagne of her dress hiked up at the hem as he led her to a side door, unlocking it with a key he fished from his pocket, and then there were stairs, cold vinyl at first then plush red carpet.

She had a jumbled impression, after another fumbling for keys, of spacious quiet, cinnamon-

coloured rugs, and being lifted on to thickly
padded cushions.

'Stay there,' the terse order came from above,
'I'll make some coffee.'

Reality came with a suddenness that shocked
her. Her eyes went round the subtly lighted room
she lay in, noting the leather bound books gleaming
richly against one wall, the dark wooded desk set
in a corner by a window, a real fireplace surrounded by a ceiling-high rock wall. Lyle's place. Oh
God—she turned her head into the yielding cush-
ion behind her, hot tears scalding her eyes.

'Oh God,' he echoed her prayer, coming silently
on her and placing a tray on the low coffee table
beside the couch. Pouring into a delicate china cup,
he thrust it towards her, saying, 'Here, drink this.
You'll feel better after it.'

Sally struggled on to one elbow, her mind and
voice entirely clear as she said, 'I'm not drunk!
Unless you think half a Martini constitutes drunk-
enness.'

'Then why the hell did you——?' The question
faded to obscurity while his eyes continued to
puzzle. 'Why, in God's name,' he went on intently,
'did you come to that party tonight?'

'I——' It was too soon to admit, even to herself,
that she had wanted to see him again, let her eyes
rest on his presence, feast on the lean hardness of a
body that was as familiar to her as her own. But
she couldn't say that, tell him that. 'Could you—
light that fire?' she asked tremulously instead, the
obvious shudder that rippled over her seeming to
get through to him. Uttering a grunt that could
have meant anything, he strode over to the fire,

bending to strike a match he took from a box on the mantel. Flames instantly leapt round the kindling and reached up to the bark-covered logs above.

As the wood kindled noisily a contrasting calm fell on Sally. What was so bad about apologising to someone you had wronged? The world gyrated on a preordained axis, admitting you had been wrong was an infinitesimal happening in the scheme of things.

'I came to the party,' she admitted haltingly, glad that Lyle had stayed across the room beside the fire, 'to say that—I'm sorry.'

Nothing but the fire made a sound in the ensuing silence until at last Lyle asked tersely, 'Sorry for what?'

'For—being what you said I was. A snob. Thinking that your book was——'

'Something academics couldn't accept as valid?' His long legs made short the distance between them, his eyes blazing yellow fire as he leaned over her. 'So when you found out I wasn't John Ainslie, that I'd written a book that's suddenly a success, I'm suddenly okay in your eyes, is that it?'

'No,' she gave back agonised, searching for words in the jumbled morass of her teeming mind. 'No, that wasn't important to me. It was just that——' her eyes flashed a green appeal up to the blaze of yellow in his, 'why didn't you tell me about Rosalie? I would have understood. All I knew was that I'd fallen in love with a married man who was obviously still in love with the wife I never knew he had.' The words that had been locked inside her poured forth now in a tortured stream. 'I thought

I could cope with the women who'd been in your life all through my college years ... you'd never asked any of them to—to marry you! Can't you see?' she stared desperately up at him, willing him to understand. 'I loved you, and then when I saw— when I looked at the dedication page on your book that night on Rock Island, I realised—I thought— that you were just filling in with me, as you had with so many others before, until you could be with the wife you loved!'

Her breasts rose and fell under the silk of her dress, and she avoided the stark downward stare of his eyes. His body seemed as tautly strung as the wires that constricted her throat, fastening round her vocal chords in a stranglehold that precluded words.

'What did you say?'

She met his eyes despairingly, anger struggling to the surface when she realised that he hadn't heard a word of what she said. 'Let me up,' she commanded, although there was nothing but the fine-spun thread of emotion between them. Her feet reached for the floor and she was standing on the luxurious thickness of the carpet several inches below Lyle's unmoving height. Her shoes ... he must have taken them off at some stage. She felt defenceless without them, and her left foot search surreptitiously across the floor for the narrow-heeled evening shoes. She moaned when Lyle's arm came down to circle her waist and drew her to the implacable hardness of his tensed body.

'Say it again,' he commanded starkly, his breath fanning warmth to her uptilted face.

'Say what?' she asked, bewildered as she lay still

against him and looked up into the faintly mad gleam in his eyes. 'I'm not going to repeat all I've said, Lyle,' she said, exasperated.

'Not all of it, just one thing,' he coaxed, though there was nothing conciliatory in the hard thrust of his jaw, the almost painful hold of his arm round her.

'I—don't know what you mean. Lyle, please——'

'You said you loved me,' he insisted, the gleam in his eyes becoming more pronounced, more yellow. 'Before you found out about Rosalie.'

The sound of his wife's name on his lips should have shrivelled any remaining love she felt for him, but it didn't. Instead, a huge compassion filled and spilled over inside her. Rosalie was of the past, a ghost who, Sally realised in a mind-shattering way, no longer existed as a vibrant entity.

'She's not there any more, is she?' she voiced her bewildered acceptance of the fact, and saw Lyle's jaw contract a few inches above her own.

'No,' he said gruffly, shifting hs body into closer alignment with Sally's, 'she's someone I knew and loved a long long time ago. She needed me at a difficult time for her.'

'And I need you too,' Sally breathed, her arms lifting to the broad outline of his shoulders, her eyes glinting the message her lips found it impossible to form. Her mouth parted under the slow assault of his, her body moulding itself to the press of his, feeling the sweet curve of hip joined to hip, thigh pressed to thigh.

It was much later when she struggled up away from his stretched body on the soft cushions of the couch and said wonderingly, 'No wonder you were

the Don Juan of the English Department! How
many girls have you brought up to your apartment?'

'None.' His fingers cupped her face, then ran up
into the thickness of her hair as he looked quizzically at her. 'I was looking for somebody like you,
a girl who wanted me for her first lover.'

Sally ran her fingers up through the curling
shortness of his chest hair, openly visible beneath
his unbuttoned shirt. 'And Magda?' she asked
wide-eyed.

'Jealous?' his voice rumbled under her.

'Madly.'

His fingers touched with sensuous lightness on
the curved bow of her mouth. 'No need,' he said
seriously. 'She and her husband, Howard, had a
few problems for a while, but they're okay now.'
He smiled, teasing. 'Howard was my buddy at college, and Magda never had eyes for anybody else,
including me.'

'Good.' Sally settled contentedly against the
shoulder she had bared for the purpose. 'Because,'
her fingers trailed with provocative menace up over
the firm outline of his mouth, 'she'd have me to
deal with if she decides otherwise!'

Lyle's lips pressed against her palm, warm and
evocative of pleasures yet unknown, and he said
huskily, 'That's a problem you'll never have,
sweetheart. No other woman will ever exist for
me.'

'Good,' Sally repeated, pulling his head down to
hers. It was a word that bore repeating.

Harlequin® Plus

A WORD ABOUT THE AUTHOR

Elizabeth Graham was born in Scotland, grew up in England, and today makes her home in British Columbia, Canada's Pacific province. Her first Harlequin, *The Girl from Finlay's River* (#2062), was published in 1977.

She is passionately devoted to her profession, which she finds a solitary one. And yet she asks, "Who can feel really lonely when a book's characters fill the mind's eye in the colorfully exciting parade of incidents and scenes that go into the weaving of a Harlequin novel?"

For Elizabeth Graham, the pure joy of creating people from the imagination cannot be equaled. "I move in a world that changes constantly," she enthuses, "and characters become so real to me that I regularly fall in love with my current hero. Only reluctantly do I relinquish him—and that's halfway through the next book."

Among Elizabeth's favorite activities is the reading of Harlequin books, and she expresses the feelings of many readers when she tells us why. "Problems," she observes, "which we all experience to a greater or lesser extent, are forgotten when I lose myself in another author's work and live for a while in her magic world. These problems are still there when I finish the story but somehow the book's happy ending spills over into my own life—and I'm better able to cope with life's ups and downs."

Take these 4 best-selling novels FREE

as advertised on TV

Yes! Four sophisticated, contemporary love stories by four world-famous authors of romance FREE, as your introduction to the Harlequin Presents subscription plan. Thrill to **Anne Mather**'s passionate story BORN OUT OF LOVE, set in the Caribbean.... Travel to darkest Africa in **Violet Winspear**'s TIME OF THE TEMPTRESS....Let **Charlotte Lamb** take you to the fascinating world of London's Fleet Street in MAN'S WORLD....Discover beautiful Greece in **Sally Wentworth**'s moving romance SAY HELLO TO YESTERDAY.

Harlequin Presents...

The very finest in romance fiction

Join the millions of avid Harlequin readers all over the world who delight in the magic of a really exciting novel. EIGHT great NEW titles published EACH MONTH!

Each month you will get to know exciting, interesting, true-to-life people .... You'll be swept to distant lands you've dreamed of visiting .... Intrigue, adventure, romance, and the destiny of many lives will thrill you through each Harlequin Presents novel.

Get all the latest books before they're sold out!

As a Harlequin subscriber you actually receive your personal copies of the latest Presents novels immediately after they come off the press, so you're sure of getting all 8 each month.

Cancel your subscription whenever you wish!

You don't have to buy any minimum number of books. Whenever you decide to stop your subscription just let us know and we'll cancel all further shipments.